my so-called family

COURTNEY SHEINMEL

SIMON & SCHUSTER BOOKS FOR YOUNG READERS
New York London Toronto Sydney

for mom & dad

SIMON & SCHUSTER BOOKS FOR YOUNG READERS
An imprint of Simon & Schuster Children's Publishing Division
1230 Avenue of the Americas, New York, New York 10020
This book is a work of fiction. Any references to historical events, real people, or real locales are used fictitiously. Other names, characters, places, and incidents are the product of the author's imagination, and any resemblance to actual events or locales or persons, living or dead, is entirely coincidental.
Copyright © 2008 by Courtney Sheinmel
All rights reserved, including the right of reproduction in whole or in part in any form.
SIMON & SCHUSTER BOOKS FOR YOUNG READERS is a trademark of Simon & Schuster, Inc.
For information about special discounts for bulk purchases, please contact Simon & Schuster Special Sales at 1-866-506-1949 or business@simonandschuster.com.
The Simon & Schuster Speakers Bureau can bring authors to your live event. For more information or to book an event, contact the Simon & Schuster Speakers Bureau at 1-866-248-3049 or visit our website at www.simonspeakers.com.
Also available in a Simon & Schuster Books for Young Readers hardcover edition.
Book design by Jeremy Wortsman
The text of this book was set in Scala.
Manufactured in the United States of America
First Simon & Schuster Books for Young Readers paperback edition
September 2009
2 4 6 8 10 9 7 5 3 1
The Library of Congress has cataloged the hardcover edition as follows:
Sheinmel, Courtney—1st ed.
22 cm.
Summary: Leah, who was conceived through a donor bank, decides that even though she loves her mother, stepfather, and stepbrother, she wants to find out if she has any other siblings, and sets out to investigate without telling anyone what she is doing.
ISBN 978-1-4169-5785-0 (hc)
[1. Stepfamilies—Fiction. 2. Brothers and sisters—Fiction. 3. Identity—Fiction.
4. Family life—New York (State)—New York—Fiction. 5. Friendship—Fiction.]
1. Title.
PZ7.S54124 My 2008
[Fic]—dc 22
2007034465
ISBN 978-1-4169-7942-5 (pbk)
ISBN 978-1-4169-8622-5 (eBook)

acknowledgments

My love and thanks first to my parents—to my mother, Elaine Sheinmel, who said this would happen before I had even written a word, and to my father, Joel Sheinmel, who cheered me on as I wrote. Thanks also to my lovely and talented sister, Alyssa Sheinmel, and to my amazing grandmothers, Diane Buda and Doris Sheinmel.

My unending thanks to my first readers—Lindsay Aaronson, Amy Bressler, Jackie Friedland, and Llen Pomeroy—whose encouragement kept me writing.

To my exceptional editor, David Gale, who believed in the manuscript and helped turn it into a real live book—my gratitude is beyond words. And thank you to Justin Chanda, Paul Crichton, Lucy Cummins, Katrina Groover, Nicole Russo, Navah Wolfe, Chava Wolin, and everyone else at Simon & Schuster who worked so hard to make this possible.

Thanks to my incredible friends, who listened all the times I wanted to talk about my book and shared the ups and downs along the way—Bob Barnard; Amanda Berlin; Maria Crocitto; Jennifer Daly; Denise, Alan, Courtney, and Morgan Fleischman; Phil, IanMichael, and the entire Getter/Liss family; Jake Glaser; Gail Glidewell; Daphne Grab; J.P. Gravitt; Allyson Jaron; Arielle Warshall Katz; Sue Lawshe; Lisa and Peter Leib; Melissa Losquadro; Sally Printz; Sascha Puritz; Jennie Rosenberg; Eric Shuffler; Katie Stein; Heidi Tanakatsubo; and Christine Whelan. Thanks also to Jenn's mom, Rose Daly, and Llen's mom, Carol Oxman, for their time and support.

I am enormously grateful to the writers who embolden me by their example, particularly to these three: Anna Quindlen, who gave a speech at my school when I was fourteen and helped me realize that I wanted to be a writer; Mary Gordon, who went from being my favorite teacher to my dear friend; and Thane Rosenbaum, who believed in me and led me to my agent.

My heartfelt thanks to Marachel and Lily Leib, for being such wonderful playmates and for saying so many smart and adorable things that I can use in my books; and to Avery and Chase Aaronson, Madden and Brody Shuffler, Abe and Asher Friedland, and Abe Pomeroy for allowing their moms the time to read.

Enormous thanks to everyone at Trident Media Group for their support, especially Lara Allen, Adam Friedstein, Dan Harvey, Phil Leibowitz, and Kasey Poserina. And finally, my deepest thanks to my agent, Alex Glass, who took a chance on a first-time writer, and made the effort infinitely worthwhile.

chapterone

We moved out of our old house on a Tuesday at the beginning of August. My stepfather, Simon, got a new job in New York City. He and Mom bought a house in Riverdale, an area just north of Manhattan, and Simon's company hired movers for us. The moving company sent three men and a woman down to our house in Maryland to help us pack up and move out.

It's funny because Mom always tells my brother Charlie and me that women can do anything. She was a single mother for a long time, so I think she wants to make sure her kids know that women are strong and independent. But the people from the moving company were totally stereotypical in terms of their jobs. The men were there to lift the heavy things, and the woman was there to talk to Mom and make sure everything stayed organized. It seemed like the main part of her job was to walk around with a clipboard and point to things.

There were only two rooms in our old house that the moving company wasn't packing up for us. The first was Mom's office. She's a writer, mostly of self-help books. Her most successful books have been how-to books for teenagers: *How to Make It Through High School* and *How to Find the Summer*

Job of Your Dreams. Anyway, Mom gets pretty territorial about her office because of her computer and her manuscripts. The woman from the moving company said she completely understood how Mom felt—I think she was probably happy to have one less room to worry about—and she gave Mom a bunch of boxes and bubble wrap.

The second room the movers weren't packing was my room. I wanted to do it myself. It's not that I like packing, and it's not even that I was worried about my stuff the way Mom was. I just wanted to box everything up myself, kind of like for closure.

When Simon found out about his new job, he and Mom went on and on about how moving is a great adventure and how it will be wonderful for the whole family. Charlie got really into it, but he's only five years old. Simon was excited because his new job is really prestigious and he's going to make more money. And moving is easy for Mom because she's a writer, so her job is portable. But for me, it was kind of different. The thing is, up until the day we moved, I'd lived in the same house for my whole life. Mom bought it the year before I was born. I always liked the way it looked—peachy pink, sandwiched between two white houses. Whenever Mom gave directions to our house, she would say, "It's the pink one on the right." I liked the way that sounded. I once told Mom that it looked like a house for girls.

In the beginning, when we lived in that house, it was a house of just girls. There were two of us: Mom and me. Mom's name is Meredith and she named me Leah, after her mother, who I never met. We're Jewish, and you're supposed to name new babies after relatives who've died. My middle name is Isabel, after Mom's dad, whose name was Isaac, even though Mom told me everyone always called him Izzy. There were no relatives on my father's side to name me after. That's because I never had a father. I know what you're thinking: You're thinking about how babies are made and how everyone has a father. But that's not exactly true.

I wasn't adopted, and I'm not talking about some miracle birth, either. My mom was thirty-three years old when she got pregnant with me. She wasn't married, even though all her friends were, and most of them were having babies. She was worried about not getting married until she was older, and then not having a baby until she was even older than that. Her parents had been on the old side when she was born, and they'd both died before she'd even turned thirty. So when her best friend announced she was pregnant, Mom decided to have a kid on her own, and she started looking into sperm banks. You know, the place where men go to donate sperm. Then women who want to have babies can go buy some sperm and get pregnant. So Mom went to the sperm bank. Some of her friends tried to talk her out of it. Even her pregnant best friend tried to talk her out of it. They said it would be harder for her to meet a man and get married if she already had a kid. But Mom says sometimes you have to trust your instincts, and her instincts told her to have a baby, so she headed to the Lyon's Reproductive Services, a sperm bank in Baltimore, Maryland.

First Mom had to choose the donor. Apparently this is not an easy thing to do. There are all sorts of things to think about, like hair color, and height, and the donor's medical history. Even though she's not religious, Mom wanted the donor to also be Jewish. She figured her parents would have been happy to know their grandchild was a purebred Jew. Frankly, I'm not sure what my grandparents would have thought about their only child going to a sperm bank to get pregnant. In the pictures I've seen, they look kind of old-fashioned. But Mom has never said anything about that. Maybe she didn't think about it because she was too busy trusting her instincts.

Anyway, there were books and books to choose from when it came to picking out a donor. When I was six years old, we had a flood in the downstairs bathroom. Water poured out of the pipe beneath the sink and soaked through everything. We had to rip all the tiles and wallpaper out, otherwise the bathroom would have gotten all moldy, and I went with Mom to pick out new wallpaper. The saleswoman handed us a few hardbound books, and we sat on a couch in a corner of the showroom and leafed through pages and pages of samples. That's how I imagine Mom picking out the donor. Except, of course, I'm not sitting there with her. But I picture her on a couch in the corner with a heavy book in her lap, and a stack of books next to her. I imagine her sitting there for hours, poring over each book very carefully, trying to find the perfect match, just like we tried to find wallpaper that would go just right with the tile and the beige rug in the hall. Mom told me that all the donors have to fill out forms about themselves. You can pay extra to see a baby picture or hear a voice sample of the donor. But no matter how much you pay, you don't get to find out the donor's name, or where he lives, or see a picture of what he looks like as a grown-up.

So Mom sifted through pages of donor forms with typed-up information—hair color, eye color, freckles, IQ score. Finally she settled on one: Donor 730. He was slender and about medium height. He was Jewish, and had green eyes and brown hair. He wasn't balding. He had olive skin, tanned easily, and said the person he admired most was his mother, who had raised him by herself. He didn't know his father. He liked skiing and reading and had gone to an Ivy League college on scholarship. His mother had been healthy her whole life, and he had never had any medical problems beyond the chicken pox. These are the things my mother picked out. I don't really feel like going into the science of it, but basically that's how she had me.

So I don't have a father; I have a donor. But when I was little, it seemed like everyone had a mommy and a daddy. I asked Mom about it, and she said that sometimes mommies don't match up with daddies, and those mommies have babies by themselves. That made sense for a while. Then my friend Abigail's mother got pregnant. One day when we were in kindergarten, and it was Abigail's mom's turn to pick us up from school, I noticed she was getting kind of fat. She could barely buckle her seat belt across her middle. From the backseat I could see her stomach pressed up against the steering wheel. Even though I knew it wasn't nice, I leaned over to ask Abigail about it. "How come your mom is so fat?" I said.

Abigail rolled her eyes. "She's not fat, silly," Abigail said. "She's having a baby."

"Oh," I said, remembering that that was what happened when women had babies. They got fat first. "How does the baby get in there, anyway?"

"Sex," Abigail said matter-of-factly.

It was a word I hadn't heard before. "What's that?" I asked.

Abigail leaned across the backseat toward me. There was something about her face that made me feel like I was about to learn something incredibly exciting. She lowered her voice. "Well," she began, "it's what moms and dads do to make babies."

I nodded, waiting to hear more, but Abigail's mother interrupted. "That's enough, Abigail," she said.

I got home and Mom met me at the front door. Mom writes every day, but she always stopped when I got home from school. I don't know what book she was working on that day when Abigail's mom dropped me off. She held the front door open for me and waved to Abigail and her mother. I shrugged off my backpack and took off my coat and scarf. "Abigail's mom is going to have a baby," I announced.

"I know," Mom said. "It's going to be a boy." I wrinkled my nose. A girl would have been better. Mom laughed. "One day you won't think boys are so bad."

We walked toward the kitchen for a snack. I always liked a snack when I got home from school. "Mom?" I said. She turned around toward me.

"What?"

"What's sex?"

I don't remember exactly how Mom explained what sex is, but I do know that as soon as she told me, something didn't quite make sense. "Then how come I don't have a daddy?" I asked. That was when Mom told me about my donor. She explained that there had been a very nice man who'd known there was a mommy out there who needed his help to have her little girl. She said even though we didn't know him, we should feel thankful to him because he had given her such an important present. We talked about the donor sometimes, when I felt sad about not having a father, like most everyone else I knew. Mom said the most important thing was that we had each other. "I know most of your friends have two parents, but not everyone does, and it's okay. Besides, you shouldn't think of it as not having a father," Mom said. "Think about how the reason you're here is because you had a donor."

But when you're a little kid, you can't exactly say that when your friends ask you where your father is. Nobody wants to be too different; at least, I didn't want to be. Over the next few years, I tried to be like everyone else. I had a best friend named Heidi, and we wore the same clothes, and I made sure I had a denim backpack because everyone had a denim backpack. My hair was long, sometimes braided, but never in pigtails. I learned to swim at camp, even though it seemed an awfully long way to the bottom of the pool and I was secretly scared of sinking in the deep end and not being able to make it back up to the surface. Whenever anyone asked me about my father, I said he lived in Europe. It seemed exotic and sophisticated, and not the bad kind of different. Europe was also far enough away that it made sense that I didn't see him. And it wasn't exactly a lie, since it was entirely possible. Who knew where my donor was? Europe seemed as likely a place as anywhere else.

That all changed in fourth grade, when Mom became friendly with my friend Heidi's mom. By that time, Mom had met Simon. I guess he didn't care that she already had a kid, because he married her and adopted me. Mom changed our last name from Hoffman to Hoffman-Ross. Then she and Simon had another kid—my brother, Charlie. One night Mom said she and Heidi's mother were going to go out for a "girls' night." I thought Heidi and I should get to go too. We were girls, after all. But Simon rented us a movie and we had to stay home with him and Charlie.

A couple of days later it was Monday. It was Mom's day to carpool, but we were running late. Mom pulled up in front of the school and Abigail and I dashed out toward our classrooms. We were in different classes. I pulled open the door to my class. Everyone was already sitting down, and our teacher, Mrs. Hould, was writing math problems on the blackboard. The kids all turned to look at me when they heard the door open. As I walked quickly toward my desk, I felt everyone staring at me. I looked across the room at Heidi. She was looking at me, but when she saw me look at her she turned her head and whispered something to the girl next to her. The girl smiled and covered her mouth with her hand as if to hold back laughter. Mrs. Hould had turned back to the blackboard, and I tried to concentrate on what she was writing. Her hand moved quickly across the board. Even though she was writing fast, her writing was straight and neat. My handwriting always looked worse when I tried to write on the blackboard, but I guess Mrs. Hould had had a lot of practice, since she was a teacher. I stared straight ahead at the numbers she was writing so I wouldn't have to see everyone looking at me.

By lunchtime, everyone knew about my donor. Mom had told Heidi's mom and Heidi's mom had told Heidi, and Heidi had told everyone. A couple of the boys started calling me "Science Experiment," as if there had been some bespectacled guy with crazy hair in a lab mixing colored liquids in glass canisters and shouting "Eureka!" when he made a baby. Even though we were supposed to eat lunch with kids from our own class, I walked my tray over to Abigail's table so I wouldn't have to talk about my donor.

"I thought you said your dad lived in Europe," Abigail said as I sat down. So it wasn't just my class that knew; it was the entire fourth grade. I swallowed hard so I wouldn't cry. I knew it shouldn't matter so much. There were two other kids in my class who didn't have fathers. Heidi's own father had just up and left one day, and they never saw him again. And a boy in my class had a father who'd died. That had to be worse than someone who may or may not live in Europe.

"I don't know where my father is," I admitted. "I don't even really have one." I stood up and left my lunch tray where it was. Suddenly I didn't feel well. My head hurt and I was dizzy. Abigail called after me, but I kept going straight to the nurse's office. I told her I felt like throwing up. They always let you go home if you are going to throw up. I lay down on the little cot in the nurse's room and listened to her call Mom. I imagined Mom sitting at her computer, writing about how to have a baby without involving a man. I closed my eyes and waited for her to come and pick me up.

The name Science Experiment stuck with me through the rest of the school year, but things died down by the time fifth grade started. Still, having a donor was the thing about me that everyone knew. Just like we all knew that Heidi's mom had gone out on a secret date with the principal. Nobody made fun of me anymore, but I always wished there were a way to go back and make sure no one knew the truth about me.

At first when Mom and Simon announced we were moving, I was really upset about having to leave. The pink house was the only place I'd ever lived. All the people I knew lived nearby. I thought about Abigail and Heidi, and everyone else I'd known for as long as I could remember. I knew the names of almost all the kids in my entire school—not just the kids in my grade. I knew all of the teachers, too. When we moved, I would have to start all over. I went into my room and lay down on my bed. I closed my eyes and tried to imagine walking into school and not knowing anybody. Everyone would be looking at me because I was the new girl, but they wouldn't know a thing about me. They wouldn't know there was anything about me that was different or strange. Lying there on my bed, I realized that moving would be a chance to be normal.

The woman from the moving company gave me boxes and bubble wrap, just like she gave to Mom. I took the posters down from the walls and packed my books up. I used the bubble wrap to wrap up the snow globes Simon brought back for me every time he returned from a busi-ness trip. It was like packing up memories. I taped up the last box and pressed it closed. Then I sat back on my bed. The room looked different, even with all my furniture still in it. You could almost tell the furniture was empty on the inside, like all the personality of the room was gone. There was a pit in my stomach, which wasn't what I thought clo-sure would feel like. It was strange how my room would be someone else's room soon, and I'd be moving into some-one else's old room.

It would be an adventure, like Mom and Simon said, and it would be a fresh start. Nobody would have to know about my donor. I could just blend in like a normal person, in a normal family of four. I stood up from my bed and went to tell Mom that I was done packing, so she could tell the movers to come in and put my boxes and furniture into the truck.

chaptertwo

At night in the new house, when everything else is quiet, you can hear the faint but steady sound of cars. Mom said the noise is because Riverdale is actually a part of New York City. It's not as noisy as Manhattan, which is the part of New York City that Simon's office is in, but it's still more crowded than the town in Maryland where the pink house is.

"It's hard to fall asleep," I complained to Mom the first morning. She was kneeling on top of the kitchen counter, lining our new cabinets with checkered paper.

"I know," she said from inside the cabinet. She turned around to look at me, and I rubbed my eyes to show her just how tired I was. "You'll get used to it, Leah. I promise."

"How do you know?" I asked her.

"I just do," she said.

The noise isn't the only thing about the new house that's different. It's bigger, too. We got rid of my old twin bed because my room was big enough for a double bed. Charlie's room isn't as big as mine, but at least it's bigger than a closet, which was about the size of his old room. Before we moved in, Simon and Mom had everything painted and put in new carpeting. When we got there, the whole house smelled new, not at all like the pink house, where everything was worn in and very cozy. The first morning that I woke up in the new house and walked downstairs for breakfast, I made a left turn instead of a right toward the kitchen. In the pink house the kitchen was to the left of the stairs. But in the new house I ended up headed toward the front door instead.

But by the time we finally finished unpacking everything and had gotten rid of all the boxes, the fresh-paint smell had started to fade. Mom was right about the noises; I got used to them and started being able to fall asleep. I was almost completely used to living there and I even started to forget things about the pink house. Like, I couldn't remember anymore what shape the doorknobs were, or whether the light switch in my bedroom was on the left- or right-hand side of the door. I also slept differently, with my arms and legs stretched out as wide as possible on my double bed. It's strange how when you get used to new things, you forget all the old things that you took for granted before.

School started a couple weeks after we finished unpacking. It was good because we didn't know anyone, so after we finished setting up the house, there really wasn't much for us to do. I was bored, and Mom was acting sort of crazy because she was writing a new book, *How to Talk So Your Parents Will Listen*. She had to get it to her editor by the end of October, and it's hard for her to work when we're home, especially when Charlie's home. But Charlie started kindergarten the same day I started eighth grade, and Mom got back to work on her book.

My homeroom teacher's name is Mrs. Levitt. You know how teachers never admit to having first names? Well, Mrs. Levitt pretends her students don't have first names either. When she calls roll in the morning, she calls us by our last names. The first day she called my name she said, "Ms. Hoffman hyphen Ross."

"Here," I said. "And it's just Hoffman-Ross. You don't have to say the hyphen." A few kids snickered. I felt myself start to blush. I hadn't meant it to sound rude. I'd just wanted to correct her pronunciation. I wondered if I should apologize, but I decided it was best to keep my mouth shut and not say anything more. So much for starting out as someone normal. I sank down in my seat and waited for homeroom to be over.

I had four classes in the morning—algebra, English, French, and biology, and they all went much more smoothly than homeroom, mostly because I didn't have to say anything. At the beginning of each class I would pull out a brand-new notebook. I love the first day of school for things like that— before notebooks are filled up and messy, when there's the possibility of everything staying perfect and easy. I took notes as the teachers outlined the curriculum for the semester. Mom had also bought me a new day planner, and I made a list, as neatly as I could, of the homework I would have for each class. I listed the classes on the left and the assignments on the right. That's the way Mom always lists things when she's writing. She'll divide the page into two columns and list the main points on the left side of the page, and then jot down ideas on the right side. When I surveyed my homework list, it seemed like an awful lot just for the first day, but we'd also started algebra at the end of seventh grade back at my old school, so at least my math homework would be pretty easy to do.

After fourth period I followed the crowd to the cafeteria. I had sort of been dreading lunch. I wasn't worried about the food or anything, but lunch is always the part of the day when you get to sit with your friends, and since I was new, I didn't have any friends to sit with. I was sure there were other new kids. It was a big enough school that there had to be some other kids who had just moved to Riverdale who didn't have anyone else to eat with. But I didn't know how to find them in the crowd, and I was worried I would end up sitting alone. I held my lunch tray and looked out at all the tables. Kids were hunched over, laughing, deep in conversation. I didn't see anyone sitting alone.

"You're the girl with the hyphen, right?" I heard a voice beside me say. I turned and saw three girls standing next to me. I recognized one of them from homeroom. She had long dark hair and the most perfectly clear skin I'd ever seen. When Mrs. Levitt had called out "Ms. Monahan," the girl had raised her hand but had kept on reading the magazine open on her desk. Now she was looking straight at me, waiting for an answer.

"Yeah," I said. Mom hates when I say "yeah." Since she's a writer, she's obsessed with things like language and grammar. She has a whole list of words she wishes I didn't say.

"I'm Avery," the girl said.

"I'm Leah," I said.

"This is Brenna, and this is Callie," Avery said. She balanced her tray on one hand and waved toward the other girls.

Brenna had dark hair like Avery, except it was very curly, and Callie was blond. They were all very pretty. I rolled their names around in my head. Avery, Brenna, and Callie—cool girl names. I wished my name were more exotic, although it could have been worse. There was a girl at my old school named Harriet, and some of the kids called her "Hairy." Parents should think about these things before they name their kids.

"Nice to meet you," I said.

"They're in a different homeroom," Avery said. She turned to them. "You should have seen it. Mrs. Levitt is so old she's practically senile, and you know how she calls everyone by their last name? So when she was calling roll this morning, when she got to Leah, she pronounced the hyphen in her last name!"

Brenna and Callie laughed. I knew it wasn't that funny a story, but I could tell Avery was the kind of person you laughed at whenever she said something she thought was funny.

Avery turned back to me. "You're new, right?"

"Yeah," I said again. I could just imagine how embarrassed Mom would have been if she'd been listening to our conversation.

"Do you have anyone to sit with for lunch?" Avery asked.

"I don't really know anyone yet," I said.

"Well, you should sit with us, then," she said. "It would suck to have to eat alone."

"Thanks," I said. I followed the girls over to a table on the far side of the room. We put our trays down, except for

Brenna, who had brought her lunch. She put down her bag and unwrapped something in tinfoil. Avery swirled spaghetti on her fork. "I hate how overcooked they always make the pasta," she said.

"You want some of this?" Brenna asked.

"No, thanks," Avery said. "I can't even really tell what it is."

"It's just steamed chicken and vegetables," Brenna said.

"No, thanks," Avery said again. She turned to me and started pointing out other kids. A few I recognized from classes I'd had earlier in the day, but mostly she pointed out older kids. "The high school kids are allowed to eat off campus for lunch, so you rarely ever see them in the cafeteria, except for the first week of school. They have this dumb rule that everyone has to eat in the cafeteria for the first week. It's about school spirit, or something cheesy like that. That's my brother, Chase," she said. Across the room I saw a guy with dark hair like Avery's, his arm draped around a blond girl. "And that's Lizzie with him. They're both seniors and they're in love or something. My dad says it's not really love. But I think he just says that because he's worried Chase is gonna want to go to whatever college Lizzie gets into. Chase is a lot smarter than Lizzie, and my parents don't want him to blow his shot at going to Yale over a girl."

"Did he get into Yale?" I asked.

"Not yet," Avery said. "He still has to apply."

"But he'll get in for sure," Brenna said. "Everyone knows that."

"Yeah," Avery said. "And everyone knows you're totally in love with him."

"Maybe," Brenna said, her face reddening. "But I just meant he'll get in because of your dad and all."

Avery turned back to me. "My dad went to Yale," she explained. "It's like his dream to have his son go there too. And Chase works really hard. He's got, like, perfect grades. My dad would flip out if he didn't get all A's."

"At least your dad puts all the pressure on Chase," Brenna said. "I'm an only child, so my parents are obsessed with my grades."

"Same with mine," Callie said.

"But you're not an only child," Brenna said.

"I practically am," Callie said.

"What are you talking about?" Brenna said. "You have a sister. You guys even share a room!"

"Yeah, and it's horrible. We barely even speak. The only way you can tell we're sisters is that we sort of look alike, and I *hate* that we look alike."

"You guys should just make up already," Avery said.

"But we're not fighting," Callie said. "We just don't like each other."

"Anyway, the point is your parents don't think of you as an only child," Brenna said.

"Whatever," Callie said. "They still want me to work hard and go to a good school. Just like I'm sure the Monahans want Avery to get good grades, even if Chase does get into Yale. Right, Av?"

Avery nodded. "What about your parents?" she asked me.

"They're okay about it, I guess," I said. "My stepfather went to Cornell. Last night he and my mom were saying how all my grades count now, and if I do well, maybe I can go to Cornell too."

"Is that why you're hyphenated?" Avery asked.

"What do you mean?"

"Because of your stepfather?"

"Oh, yeah. Ross is my stepfather's last name," I said. "He and my mom got married six years ago." I didn't tell her Hoffman was my mother's maiden name. She could just assume the Hoffman part came from my biological father. I could be like thousands of kids with a father and a stepfather. That was my plan, anyway.

"My mom's remarried too," Callie said. "I practically know my stepfather better than my real father. Does your dad live nearby at least?"

"Oh, no. He's off in Europe somewhere," I said, reciting the familiar line I usually told about my family. "I'm not exactly sure where."

"Me either," Callie said. "I mean, I don't really know where my dad is. We think he lives in Texas, but I don't know the name of the city or anything."

"That's just what it's like for me," I said. After I said it, I repeated the line over and over again in my head. My plan was working. My family was just like someone else's family. I didn't seem different or strange. For the first time in a long time, I thought maybe I could pass for normal.

chapterthree

The next Friday, Avery invited me over to her house. I had to pick up Charlie from kindergarten because Mom needed extra time writing. Charlie gets out of school about ten minutes after I do, but he doesn't start until after lunchtime. It's because the kindergarten has a morning program and an afternoon program. Mom wanted Charlie in the morning program, but it fills up quickly, and since we moved over the summer, he was signed up too late. I think Charlie is lucky to be five years old. He could sleep in late every morning if he wanted to, but somehow he's always up at the crack of dawn and downstairs eating breakfast even before my alarm clock goes off. I was like that too, when I was younger. Now I'm never awake before my alarm clock goes off.

It takes only five minutes to get over to Charlie's school from mine, but I have to leave right after my last class so I won't be late. Avery said she didn't mind coming with me, so we sprinted over to the elementary school together. Charlie's teacher was sitting by the front door of the school, shaking hands with all the kids as they left. Charlie was standing in line. "That's him," I told Avery. "The one with the striped red shirt."

"Oh, he's so cute," Avery said. "He looks so mature, like a little man." "Mature" seemed like the wrong word for Charlie. After all, he's just a little kid and he's short for his age, which makes him look younger than most of the other kids. He hates that. I watched him shake Mrs. Trager's hand. He looked so serious as he pumped his hand up and down. Then he turned to face the crowd of parents and babysitters gathered to pick up the kids. When he saw me, he grinned his lopsided grin. There was something white pinned to his shirt, probably one of those letters that teachers attach to the kids so they don't forget to give it to their parents. It flapped in the breeze as he ran toward me.

"Leah!" Charlie said.

I introduced Charlie to Avery. Suddenly shy, he leaned against me. I nudged him, hoping he would shake her hand, but he stayed glued to my side. I pulled at the paper on his shirt.

"That's for Mom and Dad," Charlie said. He was speaking softly, and I pretended I couldn't hear him.

"What?"

"It's for Mom and Dad," he said again, just a little more loudly. "Mrs. Trager pinned letters to everyone's shirts so we wouldn't lose them."

I unhooked the safety pin and put the letter into my backpack. "Guess what?" I said. "I'm going to Avery's house now, and she invited you, too."

"Really?" Charlie asked. He loves when I include him in things. It's the best part of him being so much younger. Sometimes it's annoying when he wants to hang out with me all the time. But then there are the times when he comes into my room at night and sits on my bed and just watches me. No matter what I'm doing, even if I'm just doing my homework, he sits there captivated. I get worried that as he gets older, he won't think I'm so special.

"Yup," I told him. "You get to come."

"Hey, Charlie," Avery said, bending down so she was at his eye level, "do you like chocolate chip cookies?" Charlie shrugged, still shy. "Well," Avery continued, "I was going to say we could make them at my house, but maybe you don't like chocolate."

"I like chocolate," Charlie said softly.

"I don't know," Avery said.

"I do, I do like chocolate!" Charlie said, loudly now. "My favorite movie is even *Willy Wonka and the Chocolate Factory*."

"It is?" Avery said. She threw her head back and began to sing, "Oompa loompa doopidy doo." Charlie giggled. "Come on, sing with me."

"You're crazy," Charlie said.

"I know," Avery said. "Now sing."

"I've got another puzzle for you," Charlie sang.

"You sound great," Avery told him. She extended a hand toward him and he took it. Then he reached up for my hand, and we walked like that, all three of us connected, to Avery's house.

Avery's mom was home when we got there. She had the same dark hair and clear skin as Avery, and she told me I could call her by her first name, which is Lori. We dropped our bags in the front hall and went straight into the kitchen because Charlie could hardly wait to get started on the cookies.

Lori followed us. She opened up cabinets. "I have no idea if we even have flour and sugar and all that."

"We're okay, Mom," Avery said.

"Good," Lori said. "I don't have time to help you anyway. I have to pack because Dad and I are going away for the weekend."

"You're going away?" Avery asked.

"Uh-huh," Lori said. "Some bigwig from Dad's office decided to invite us to his country house in East Hampton. I'm betting we were invited because another couple canceled, but you know Dad—he never turns down an invitation to mingle with those corporate guys. I know it's the last minute, so I hope you're okay with it. I already talked to Chase, and he said he'd keep an eye on you."

"Mom," Avery said. "I'm practically fourteen. I don't need Chase to keep an eye on me."

"Fine," Lori said. "Then you can keep an eye on him and make sure he doesn't have any wild parties or burn the house down. Also, we have those tickets for the Broadway matinee of *The Lion King* tomorrow, so you can each bring a friend. Chase is bringing Lizzie, of course—don't tell your father." Lori turned to me. "Have you ever seen a Broadway show?" she asked.

"No," I said. "We just moved to New York. I saw a couple plays in Baltimore, though."

"Well, now Avery has an extra ticket for you," Lori said. "Trust me, there's nothing like a show on Broadway." I hoped Avery wouldn't be upset that her mom had invited me to use the extra ticket. Maybe she'd wanted to bring Brenna or Callie.

Lori said she'd be upstairs packing if we needed her.

"So can you come?" Avery asked.

"I think I'm free," I said. "Is that okay?"

"Yeah, of course," Avery said.

"I'm free too," Charlie piped up. "Do I get to go? *The Lion King* is my favorite!"

"I thought *Willy Wonka* was your favorite," Avery said.

"They're both my favorites," Charlie told her.

"Well, you're lucky because you get to watch them both when we get home," I told him. Sometimes the best way to deal with kids is to distract them. I knew if I mentioned watching the movies, Charlie would forget all about the play.

"Will you watch with me?" he asked.

"Sure," I said. "Now help me put the chocolate chips into a bowl."

"Oh, cool," Charlie said. I opened the bag and handed it to him. He poured the chocolate chips in slowly and carefully. He spilled only a couple and I let him eat the ones that didn't make it into the bowl.

When Charlie and I got home that evening, we carried a package of fresh-baked cookies. They were still warm from the oven, and I could feel them through the tinfoil as I carried them into the house. "I think they're still gooey," I told Charlie.

"Can I have one?" he asked. He'd already had three cookies plus a few chocolate chips back at Avery's house.

"You'd better ask Mom and Dad," I told him. Even though I call Simon by his first name when I'm talking to him, I call him Dad when I'm speaking to Charlie.

"Mom! Dad!" Charlie called.

Mom and Simon told Charlie he'd have to wait until after dinner for another cookie. I went upstairs to drop my backpack in my room and get started on my homework. I know it's kind of dorky, but I like to at least get started on my homework on Fridays so I'll have more of the weekend free. I pulled out my math notebook. There was enough time to finish my math work sheet before dinner.

Later on, when Mom called me for dinner, I picked up the letter from Charlie's teacher that I'd stuffed into my backpack and headed downstairs. There was a box of pizza on the table and paper plates instead of our regular dishes. Mom never cooks when she's on a deadline, which is fine with me since pizza is one of my favorite meals. "Don't get too used to this," Mom said. "My book is almost done."

I sat down in the same chair I always used. Right when we'd moved in, I'd claimed it for myself. It's the chair that's positioned kind of in the corner of the room, up against the back wall. If I tilt my head in the right way, I can see the screen of the television in the next room, and no one can even tell. Sometimes Mom and Simon forget to turn it off, and then I can watch TV while I eat, although I have to be careful not to look like I'm watching TV. Technically I'm not allowed to watch TV during a family meal. Now I could see *The Lion King* movie playing in the other room. Charlie must have started watching it without me.

We each took a slice of pizza, and Mom reached over to help Charlie cut his into bite-size pieces. "You guys got a letter from Charlie's teacher," I said. Since Mom's hands were busy, I handed it to Simon.

"What's it say? What's it say?" Charlie asked, bouncing up and down in his seat.

"Settle down," Mom told him. She slipped a piece of pizza into his mouth. "So?" she said to Simon.

Simon read the letter to himself. "Chuck," he said. Simon's the only one who calls Charlie "Chuck." "It looks like this month is Family Month at school and your class is going to do a big project on families."

"I know," Charlie said. "Mrs. Trager told us. First I have to interview you and Mom, and then I have to interview Leah, and then I get to make a big poster of the whole family. It's called a family tree. Each person is a branch." Charlie held his arms out like a tree. "Like this. I'm a branch. Isn't that funny?" He threw his head back and laughed. Mom says he has the deep-throated laugh of her father. I remembered Avery saying Charlie looked like a little man.

"You've got two branches there," Mom said. She traced her fingers along each of his arms, and then poked him in the belly. "And a trunk," she added.

"How many branches on my family tree?" Charlie asked.

"Well," Simon said, "there are four for us. And then Grandma Diane and Grandpa Willie, and Uncle Eric and Aunt Amy and all your cousins."

"What about my other grandma and grandpa? Do they get branches even though they're dead?"

"Yes," Mom said. "Grandma Leah and Grandpa Izzy get branches too."

I pictured Charlie's tree in my head, with all the branches

from Simon's side of the family on one side of the trunk, and all the branches from Mom's side of the family on the other side. I was glad I didn't have to make that kind of thing when I was in kindergarten, or else it would have been a lopsided tree. Things like that would always be easier for Charlie, and I was jealous. I bet he would never have to worry about his family being normal.

"Are you going to help me with the poster?" Charlie asked Mom.

"Leah can help you," Mom said. "She's a much better artist than I am." It's true. Mom may write well, but she never illustrates anything she's written. She says she's just not creative that way. But drawing is one of my favorite things to do.

"Oh, yeah," Charlie said. "Leah will help me."

"Oh, *yes*," Mom corrected him.

Charlie turned to me. "Can we start tomorrow?" he asked. "Daddy can take us to buy poster board. Right, Daddy? It's Saturday, so you don't have work."

"Sure thing, Chuck," Simon said. "And we can get started on those interviews, too."

"I could interview everyone at the family reunion!" Charlie said. Simon's family always has a big reunion in the spring. There are a lot of people in the Ross family, and they all sit around on picnic benches and pinch all the little kids' cheeks. Simon's brother wears a big chef's hat and barbecues about a thousand hot dogs and hamburgers. Then all the cousins run around and chase one another, and Mom says how fabulous it is to be married to Simon and be a part

of such a big and wonderful family. Of course I'm supposed
to agree with her about that. But the truth is that I don't
really like going, since Simon's family clearly likes Charlie
more than they like me. After all, he's Simon's real kid—the
one they're actually related to.

"Well, the reunion's not for a few months," Simon said.
"But you can interview everyone over the phone. You know
how Grandma loves to talk to you on the phone."

"Uh-huh," Charlie said. "And then Leah and me can
make the poster tomorrow."

"Leah and *I*," Mom said. "And yes, you can."

"Except I'm busy tomorrow," I said.

"What are you doing?" Mom asked.

"My friend Avery invited me to a Broadway show tomorrow," I told her. "Her parents can't use the tickets, so I'm
going with Avery and her brother, Chase. He's driving us
into the city."

"Is the show at night?" Simon asked.

"No, it's during the day," I said. "Her mom said it was
a matinee."

"So you'll be home for dinner?" he asked.

"I don't know," I said. "I think we're going out for dinner
after the show." Actually, I hadn't even thought about dinner, but I figured it was safer to tell Mom and Simon that I
wouldn't be home.

"I don't know about this," Mom said. "You barely know
your way around Riverdale. I'm not sure I want you wandering around Manhattan."

"Mom, please," I said. "We're not going to wander.

Chase's going to drive us straight to the theater. He's a senior and he's a really good driver." I had no idea what kind of driver Chase was, but I didn't think Avery's parents would let Chase take the car if he were a bad driver.

"What do you think?" Mom asked Simon.

"I think we should let her go," Simon said. "As long as she's home before curfew." I never had a curfew when we lived in Baltimore, but then again I'd never gone into a major city without my parents or other grown-ups around.

"So, what's my curfew?" I asked.

Mom and Simon said they would have to discuss it and they would tell me in the morning.

The next morning Mom and Simon told me I could go as long as I was back in Riverdale by nine thirty. "I don't care if you hang out at Avery's house after that, but I don't want you guys in Manhattan so late," Mom said. "That should give you plenty of time to go to the matinee, get an early dinner, and drive back to Riverdale. Deal?"

"It's a deal," I told her. "Thanks."

"And you'll take your cell phone? And you'll call when you get there? And you'll call on your way home?"

"Yes, yes, and yes," I told her. I would have agreed to just about anything because I was so excited—my first trip into Manhattan without my parents and my first Broadway show all in one day. Simon handed me forty dollars and told me to have fun. I went upstairs to get ready. Chase and Avery would be on their way to pick me up soon.

chapterfour

I wanted to wear jeans, but Mom said since I was going to Broadway I should try to look a little nicer. She thought I should wear a skirt, but we compromised and I put on my black pants that stop just above my ankles, and one of my nicer-looking T-shirts. I went back downstairs to wait for Avery. Mom followed me down and kept reminding me to take my cell phone and call her when we got into Manhattan. I heard a car pull up outside and then a horn honking. "I bet that's Avery," I said.

"I'll walk you out," Mom said. I think sometimes she gets so used to Charlie being a little kid that she thinks of me as one too.

"I don't need you to walk me out, Mom," I told her. "I'm not a baby."

"I know, I know," she said. "I just want to make sure you'll be home by nine thirty."

The horn honked a second time. "I've got to go," I said. "I'll tell them about the curfew and I'll call you later. I promise." I pecked her on the cheek and ran out to the car. It was a sports car, and Chase had to get out of the driver's seat and move the seat forward so that I could squeeze into the back with Avery. The music was blaring—much louder than anything Simon or Mom had ever played in the car, and I knew it was better that Mom had stayed inside. I could see her peeking through the window in the front hall, but at least she couldn't hear anything.

Avery introduced me to Chase and Lizzie, who was sitting next to Chase. I noticed that everyone was wearing jeans, and I wished I were too. Avery had sunglasses pushed to the top of her head like a headband. Mom never likes me to wear my sunglasses like that because it stretches them out and then they can fall off when you're actually trying to wear them as sunglasses. "By the way," Avery said, "next time you see my mom, don't mention we took the sports car. We were supposed to take my mom's sedan."

"I love this car," Lizzie said.

"My father loves it too," Chase said. "It's his midlife crisis car."

"Do you think there's a chance he'll let you take it to college next year?" Lizzie asked.

"Only if I'm at Yale," Chase said.

"Oh, forget Yale," Lizzie said. "I hope this year lasts forever. I don't want to even think about you being at Yale next year."

"You're the one who brought it up," Chase said. He reached over to turn the music up even louder. Lizzie turned away from Chase and looked out the window. We pulled onto the highway.

I could see the clock on the dashboard from the backseat. It said 2:14. "The play starts at three, right?" I asked. I had to talk louder than usual because of the music. Simon had told me it takes about a half hour to get into Manhattan from Riverdale. But then we'd have to park the car and walk to the theater and find our seats. I hoped we wouldn't be late. I'm the type of person who's always on time for things.

"It doesn't matter," Avery said. "There's been a change of plans."

I was about to ask what she meant when Chase said, "That's right. We're going to Lizzie's aunt's house instead."

"How come?" I asked.

"Because she's not home," Lizzie said.

"But what about the play?" I asked.

"Oh, come on," Chase said. "It's *The Lion King*. Do you really want to see it? It's practically a cartoon."

"No," I said, "I guess not." I didn't say it out loud, but *The Lion King* is one of the movies I actually like watching with Charlie.

"What if your mom asks about the play?" I whispered to Avery. Well, it wasn't really a whisper; it was more like my regular voice that sounded like a whisper over the music.

"It's no big deal," Avery said. "We've all seen the movie, right?" I nodded. "Well, how different could it be?"

Simon was right about how long it takes to get to Manhattan. We got off the highway, and Lizzie turned the music down so she could give Chase directions. "Make a left on Eighty-sixth Street and then a right on Lexington. Now make another right. There, it's the building there on the right." We had to drive around the corner a couple times to find a parking spot, and then we walked back around the block to Lizzie's aunt's building. There was a doorman out front and a sign that said ALL VISITORS MUST BE ANNOUNCED. I thought maybe he wouldn't let us in since we didn't live in the building and Lizzie's aunt wasn't home for him to announce us to, but he smiled and tipped his hat when he saw us coming. "Well, if it isn't my favorite visitor," the doorman said.

"Hey, Larry," Lizzie said.

"Your aunt's not home, you know," Larry said.

"I know," Lizzie said. "I have the key." She pulled a ring of keys out of her pocket and swung them like a hula hoop around her finger. Larry held the door open for us, and we walked into the building. Lizzie pressed the button for the elevator.

Now that we were officially in Manhattan, I knew I had to call home and check in, but I felt kind of dumb about it. After all, no one else seemed concerned with checking in with their parents. So when we got upstairs, I went into the bathroom and called Mom from my cell phone so no one would see me and I wouldn't feel like a baby. The answering machine picked up and I left a quick message that we'd made it into Manhattan and that I'd call again on our way home. I flushed the toilet and washed my hands even though I hadn't really used the bathroom, and then I walked back out into the living room. Avery was sitting on an ottoman. Chase was sitting on the floor with his knees up, and Lizzie was on the couch with her legs outstretched, her feet resting on Chase's knees. I sat down on the other side of the couch, wondering what we were going to do now that we were there.

"I'm starving," Chase said.

"Okay, I'll check out the kitchen," Lizzie said. She lifted her feet from Chase's knees. I watched him absently reach out and pat her ankle as she walked past him. A few seconds later she came back out. "There's absolutely nothing to eat," she said. "I guess they threw everything out before they went away. But we could go out and get something to eat if you want."

"No, that's all right," Chase said. "How about a tour of the rest of the apartment?"

I started to get up but Avery stayed seated, and I realized we weren't invited. Chase trailed behind Lizzie, and after a few seconds I heard a door close down the hall. "Well, I'm still hungry," Avery said. "I didn't even eat lunch. Did you?"

"I ate at home," I said.

"I think I'm getting my period," Avery said. "I'm starving even though I feel bloated. Do you have yours?"

"Not right now," I told her.

"I meant, do you have it at all?" Avery asked. I nodded. The truth was I had only gotten it once, a few months ago. I wasn't even sure it really was my period because it was just spotting. It didn't even look like blood—it was more rust-colored than red, and it only lasted a couple of days. Mom said it could take a while before I actually got my period regularly, but she bought me a box of maxi pads to keep in my bathroom just in case. So far I hadn't used them.

"We could go out and see if there's anything to eat," Avery said. "You could get a snack or a soda or something."

"I don't know," I said. "What if Chase and Lizzie come out and can't find us?"

"We'll leave a note," Avery said. "We won't be gone for

too long, and they'll be in there for a while. Anyway, I can't think of anything better to do. Can you?"

I knew Mom and Simon probably wouldn't have approved of Avery and me walking around Manhattan, but I couldn't think of anything else for us to do either. Besides, we were teenagers. I had been allowed to walk around our neighborhood in Maryland on my own, and I'd been allowed to walk around in Riverdale on my own. Avery didn't seem to think Manhattan was any different. "You're right," I said. "Let's go."

Avery wandered into the kitchen to find a pen and paper to write a note to Chase. We checked the door to make sure it wouldn't lock behind us, since Lizzie had taken the key with her, and we headed downstairs. Larry tipped his hat again when he saw us, and held open the door.

We hadn't turned on any of the lights in the apartment. The sun had been streaming through the blinds, so it hadn't felt like we had been sitting in the dark, but when we got outside, the sun was blinding and I had to squint. Avery pulled her sunglasses down from the top of her head. "I love this time of year, don't you?" she asked. She held out her arms and twirled around. I thought her sunglasses would fall off, but they didn't. "It almost still feels like summer, but not as humid. What's that called again?"

"I think it's called Indian summer," I told her.

"Right," she said. She spun around again. "I feel like dancing, don't you?"

"No," I said. "Not here in the middle of the street."

"Why not?"

"Well," I said, "people could see us, for one thing."

"Oh, Leah," Avery said. "Don't be so uptight. You can't spend your time worrying about what other people think. I never do." I wondered if that meant I shouldn't have worried about whether everyone thought I was a baby for calling Mom, or if I shouldn't have cared if Mom was worried about me. Avery grabbed my hand and spun herself around me. From down the block I heard Larry whistle. Avery took a bow and turned back to me. "You see?" she said. "It's no big deal." I noticed that Avery said that a lot.

We found a deli a couple blocks away and bought chips and soda. Avery said she thought if we kept walking west, we'd hit Central Park. I didn't know which way was east and which was west. Mom had said she didn't want me wandering around Manhattan. I followed Avery since she seemed to know where to go, even though I remembered hearing that Central Park could be dangerous. I had heard of people getting attacked or kidnapped in the park. I pictured a man in a dark coat and a ski mask. I pictured his arms reaching out from behind a tree and pulling us into the woods. Maybe he would have a car parked back there. He would shove us into the car and drive us away, and no one would know where to look for us. Our parents thought we were at a play, and we hadn't even told Chase we were going to Central Park.

Avery was skipping down the block. "Come on, Leah," she called. I felt stupid for worrying about things that I knew probably weren't going to happen, but maybe if you worry about them, you can make sure they don't come true. Sort of like jinxing it. I thought to myself, *Please don't let us be kidnapped*, and then I raced to catch up with Avery.

chapterfive

We didn't meet up with any kidnappers in Central Park. Instead we picnicked on the grass next to a huge building that Avery said was a famous museum. Later on we headed back to the apartment. Avery and I flopped onto the couch. Chase and Lizzie were still nowhere to be seen. "We were gone for so long," I said. "What do you think they're doing?"

"Making out or making up or something," Avery said.

"What do you mean?" I asked. "They weren't fighting."

"In the car," she explained. "Chase said something about Yale and Lizzie got upset."

"She didn't seem to be upset for too long," I said.

"I know," Avery said. "But this is why my dad's so worried about Yale. Chase always feels guilty about maybe having to leave Lizzie behind next year. He barely thinks about anything else. It's like Lizzie is the only person in the world."

"Oh," I said.

"Anyway, I'm bored," Avery said. "I saw a computer down the hall. Let's go check e-mail."

Mom has always been protective of her computer. She gets nervous that someone will press the wrong button and then whatever book she's working on will disappear. When she's on a deadline, no one is allowed to go near her computer, not even Simon. Mom even got me my own computer so I wouldn't have to use hers. I didn't think we should use Lizzie's aunt's computer in case Lizzie's aunt was like Mom, but I didn't say anything to Avery. It's confusing not to worry about what people are thinking—should you not worry about saying anything, or not worry about the thing you were going to say to begin with?

Avery logged into her e-mail. "Hey, look," she said. "Brenna e-mailed me new ringtones from *America's Next Rock Star*. Do you watch that show?"

"No," I said. "I'm not really into the reality shows."

"I know. They're awful," Avery said. "Chase hates them too. He says they're a way for the networks to make a lot of money without having to pay all the actors or come up with anything creative. It probably means I'm stupid, but I love them anyway. I wish I'd brought my cell phone."

"I have mine," I said. I pulled it out of my pocket and handed it to Avery.

"But you don't watch it," she said.

"It's okay," I told her. "If I hate them, I'll just switch it back."

"You won't hate them," Avery said. "I swear. Some of the singers are really good." Avery flipped my phone open and dialed into the ringtones. "I'm going to program in my number, and Brenna's and Callie's numbers. Then I can program this to play different songs depending on which one of us is calling. Okay?"

"Sure," I said.

"Oh, this is so cool," Avery said. "They have this song that Luci Williams sang last week. It was her farewell song, actually, because she was voted off, which was totally unfair, by the way. She is so, so talented. I was practically crying when she sang!"

Avery downloaded the song by Luci Williams, and then she downloaded a couple of other songs to play when Brenna and Callie called. We called Brenna and Callie so they could call us back and make sure it worked. By the time we'd finished, Chase and Lizzie had come back out. "Are you guys ready?" Chase asked.

"For what?" Avery asked.

"Dinner," Chase said. "Some kids who graduated last year are in the city, and we're going to meet up. Come on."

We had to drive to another part of Manhattan to get to the restaurant. When we got into the car, I saw the clock on the dashboard said 7:03. If we'd gone to the play, we would probably already have been at a restaurant eating. Maybe we would've even been waiting for the check and getting ready to head back to Riverdale.

"How far away is the restaurant?" I asked.

"Uptown, near Columbia," Chase said. "I guess about fifteen minutes."

I calculated in my head—fifteen minutes to get there and thirty minutes to drive back to Riverdale. That left us nearly an hour and forty-five minutes to eat and get back to Riverdale by nine thirty.

The restaurant was called Nacho Mama's. We drove

around and around again looking for a parking place nearby, but we couldn't find one. Finally Chase pulled into a lot. Chase's friends had already gotten a table.

"Hey, man," Chase said. One of the guys sitting at the table stood up and gave Chase a sort of half hug, half pat on the back.

"Chase, man," the guy said. "What'll it be?" The guy held up a pitcher of beer. I wondered how come they had beer on the table—I didn't think they were twenty-one. Maybe they had fake IDs. Mom would kill me if she knew.

"No thanks, man, nothing for me," Chase said. "I'm driving."

Avery leaned over to me. "They all call each other 'man.' We should start counting because I'll bet they'll say 'man,' like, a thousand times in the next couple of hours."

The waiter dropped off menus for the four of us. Lizzie asked Chase's friend to pour her a drink. She sat up against Chase and he put his arm around her. Chase's friend offered Avery and me beer too.

"No way, man," Chase said. "It's my little sister. She's, like, twelve."

"I'm thirteen," Avery said.

"Whatever," Chase said.

"Sorry, man," the guy said.

"See what I mean," Avery whispered to me.

It took a while for everyone to decide what to get, but we finally ordered our food. Avery and I decided to split a plate of nachos and a quesadilla. The guy who had offered us the beer turned out to be named Ryan. Chase knew him because they had both played on the tennis team the year before.

"Come to Columbia, man," Ryan said. "We could use someone with your backhand."

"I don't know," Chase said. "It's a little too close to home. Besides, I haven't been playing as much this year."

"Oh no, Chase, it's perfect," Lizzie said. "I could apply to NYU. I bet I'd get in, and then we'd only be a subway ride away from each other."

Chase shrugged. "I'll think about it, man. Definitely," he said.

I looked across the table at Lizzie. She was still squeezed up against Chase, and she picked up her beer and took a long sip. She held her glass to her mouth for so long that I wondered if she was actually drinking or just staring into it. I sort of felt sorry for her. I watched her hand as she finally moved the glass from her lips back to the table, her fingers gripped tightly around the handle. Chase rubbed his hand up and down her arm. "Hey, guys," Ryan said. "Chin up. The food's here."

The food was great. Avery and I devoured the nachos and most of the quesadilla, but it seemed to take everyone else a really long time to finish eating. Maybe because they were all talking and drinking, too. I had no idea how late it was. I tried to count backward and figure out how much time it had taken to drive to Columbia and park the car and walk to the restaurant and order the food and eat. Probably more than the time I had allotted for it. I pulled my cell phone out of my pocket and flipped it open to see the time. 9:42. "I'll be right back," I told Avery. "I'm just gonna run to the bathroom."

The waiter pointed me to the back of the restaurant. I

walked in and dialed home. I leaned up against one of the sinks and listened to the phone ring.

Mom answered. "Leah?" she said.

"Yes, it's me," I told her. "I'm sorry to be calling so late."

"Where are you?" Mom asked.

"I'm with Avery," I said. "You said it was all right to stay out past nine thirty as long as we were back in Riverdale."

"Yes, yes," Mom said. "That's fine. So, where are you?"

"At Avery's," I said as my phone beeped.

"What?" Mom asked.

"I'm at Avery's house, but I think my phone's about to die," I said. I guess downloading all those ringtones had used up most of the battery.

"I'll call you back at Avery's," Mom said.

"Um, I don't know the number," I said. "And Avery is in the other room."

"I have it," Mom said. "It's in the school directory."

"You can't call," I said. My phone beeped again. It was about to disconnect me.

"Why not?" I didn't answer. "Leah," Mom said, "where are you?"

I took a deep breath. There wasn't enough time to make something up.

"Leah, where are you?" she said again. This time it didn't sound like a question. It sounded like an accusation.

"We're in Manhattan," I said.

I heard Mom breathe in, about to say something. Then the line went dead. I snapped my phone shut and shoved it back into my pocket. Even though I was alone in the bathroom, my cheeks flushed the way they did when people were watching me. I looked into the mirror and waited for them to turn back to their normal color.

"Everything okay?" Chase asked when I got back to the table.

Of course it wasn't okay. My mother was probably planning how long she would ground me. I wished we were home, and I felt like a baby. No matter what Avery said, I wasn't very good about not worrying what other people thought of me. I couldn't help it. Anyway, it was easy for Avery to say. She had a normal family; she was popular; she had parents who let her and her brother go into Manhattan on their own. If I told Chase what had happened, he would think I was a baby too. "Everything's fine," I said.

We finally left the restaurant and walked back to the parking lot to get the car. It didn't take long to get home from Columbia. Avery asked me if I wanted to sleep over, and I seriously considered it. I would be in trouble no matter what, so why not delay it until the morning? But then I had visions of Mom and Simon calling the police and reporting me as a missing person, lost somewhere in Manhattan. "No," I said. "I should just go home."

Simon and Mom were sitting at the dining room table when I walked in the door. "Leah," Mom said. "It's nearly eleven o'clock."

"I'm sorry," I said.

"You're sorry? Are you kidding me?" Simon asked. "We've been trying to call you back for over an hour. We were worried sick."

"I'm really sorry," I said. "My phone died." I pulled it out of my pocket and held it up to show them.

"Your phone has nothing to do with your being in Manhattan until eleven o'clock," Mom said.

"What did you want me to do? We were at dinner, and the food took a really long time. I called you as soon as I saw how late it was."

"And then you lied," she said.

"I didn't want you to be upset," I said.

"Well, that turned out really well for you, didn't it?" she said.

"It's not like I did anything unsafe," I told them. "I was with Avery and her brother the whole time. We were at a restaurant. We weren't wandering around."

"I don't care where you were," Mom said. "You weren't where you promised you would be." She looked over at Simon.

"That's right," he said. "But from now on you're going to be exactly where we tell you to be."

"What do you mean?" I asked.

"You're grounded," Simon said. "Until further notice. That means you come straight home after school. You do your homework. And no cell phone calls unless they're to Mom or me."

Even though I knew it was coming, it still felt like they'd kicked me in the stomach. I was just starting to make new friends. But Avery already had Brenna and Callie. If I couldn't hang out with her, she would probably forget all about me. "Please," I said. "I didn't mean for this to happen. You're going to make me lose my friends."

"You should have thought of that before," Mom said.

"But I did," I said. "I really was thinking about you guys the whole time. I wanted to come home, but we were stuck in a restaurant. It's not my fault!"

"Keep your voice down," Mom said.

"Chase and Avery don't have a curfew," I said.

"Maybe these aren't the kinds of friends you should be hanging out with anyway. They seem a bit wild. Letting your kids drive into Manhattan by themselves without a curfew is crazy to me."

"You don't know them at all," I said. "You're the one who's crazy!"

"Mommy!" Charlie called.

"Oh, Leah," Mom said. "Now you woke your brother."

"I don't care," I said as Mom got up from the table to head upstairs. I heard Charlie calling her again.

"I'm coming," Mom called.

"What's gotten into you, Leah?" Simon said. "All you had to do was call. If you couldn't get home, we could have figured something out. I would have come to get you. We made it so easy on you."

"Easy on me?" I said. "You have no idea how hard it is to be me. You don't even care about me."

"I'm your father," Simon said.

"You're not my real father," I said. My voice caught and I was afraid I was going to cry. I turned toward the stairs. Simon called after me and I turned back around. "You don't know anything at all!" I told him. I felt the tears start, and I stomped upstairs. There was always something about me that was different. First I didn't have normal parents, and now the ones I had were ruining my life. I just wanted to be like everyone else.

I slammed my bedroom door shut. It's not like I had to worry about waking up Charlie. I knew Mom was sitting with him, probably telling him another bedtime story. She's really good at making them up. When I was little, I liked going to bed because it meant she would sit there with me and tell me story after story until I fell asleep. "This is the one about Princess Leah," Mom would say, pronouncing my name just like the princess in *Star Wars*. It all seemed like a really long time ago. Now I felt too angry to go to bed. I flicked the switch to turn my computer on, and then I clicked on the button for the Internet. I knew exactly what website I wanted to go to. I typed in the address and watched it open up on the screen. Across the top in blue block printing were the words "Lyon's Reproductive Services." I had found the website a few months before. I never told anyone about it, not even Mom. I just wanted to see where I'd come from. This time there was a link at the bottom that I'd never noticed before. It almost felt like alarms should have sounded when I saw it. But aside from my breaths and my heart pounding in my ears, the room was silent. Sometimes you know you're about to change your life with just one little movement, like the last time I turned off the light in my bedroom at the pink house, or when I saw Mom slip a ring onto Simon's finger on their wedding day. That's how I felt when I clicked the link to "Lyon's Sibling Registry." I moved the mouse so the cursor was over the words and I pressed my finger down.

chaptersix

That first night, when I clicked on the words, an online registration form popped up, with spaces where you had to fill in your credit card information. I realized that you had to pay in order to use the website, and I thought of the credit card in my wallet—the "emergency only" credit card that Mom and Simon had given me the year before. It's not really my credit card—it has my name on the front, but it's connected to their credit card account, and the bills go to them. I'd used it only a few times, and always with permission. If only you could send cash through the computer. I could use the money left over from what Simon had given me, or some that I'd saved from babysitting, and then Mom and Simon would never find out. But the Lyon's Sibling Registry accepted credit cards only. My eyes moved back and forth between the screen and my backpack. My wallet was in the front pocket, the credit card inside of it. I began to reach for it, but then I heard Simon's and Mom's voices in the hall, and turned to shut down my computer in case they were about to come in and yell at me some more.

Still, I couldn't stop thinking about what I might have found if I'd just entered in the credit card information. I could have half siblings anywhere, even in New York. Even right here in Riverdale. I started searching the faces of other kids in school to see if they looked like me. The problem is, when you're searching for similarities between you and other people, all the features sort of blend together. Two eyes, a nose, and a mouth. Suddenly everyone looked like me, at least enough to be a possible sibling.

I hadn't really ever thought of having siblings before. I mean except for Charlie. Over the years, since Mom first told me about my donor, I'd sometimes looked at men and considered their features to see if maybe I could find someone who might be my donor. Once, when I was about nine years old, I saw someone I was sure was my donor. Mom had just written *How to Study for the SATs*, which I think is her most boring book ever, but it sold a lot of copies. Anyway, she was giving a speech at a bookstore in Baltimore, and there was a man there, sitting two rows behind me. I spotted him accidentally, when someone coughed and I turned to see who it was. And there he was. He lowered his hand from his mouth, and I saw that he had green eyes and brown hair and olive skin, just like my donor did. But it was more than that. There was something about the spacing between his eyes, the way he smiled when he saw me looking at him, with the right side of his mouth lifted up a little bit higher than the left. Mom didn't smile like that, but I did. I stayed twisted around in my seat and stared at him instead of watching Mom.

Mom finished speaking, and I turned in my seat to watch the man walk up to get a signed copy of her book. He was all alone. It was strange that he was there without one of his kids, since it wasn't exactly a book for grown-ups, and then I knew he must have come because he knew about me and wanted to find me. I got up and walked over to the table where Mom was signing. I stood behind her, not on the line like everyone else, so that he would know for sure that it was me. But when it was his turn to get his book signed, he didn't say anything about being a donor. He just said, "My niece loves your books, and she's applying to college in the fall." Mom asked his niece's name, and I leaned over her shoulder and watched her write: "For Jackie, with best of luck on the SATs, Meredith Hoffman-Ross." Mom once told me that before her first book came out, she practiced her signature over and over again, imagining how it would be when she had to give autographs. It must have worked, because her handwriting was neat and even, just like a teacher's. She closed the book and handed it back to the man. He smiled and thanked her, then turned to walk away. He didn't say anything about me. I wondered if maybe he was too scared. Or maybe he thought it was just the wrong time, with so many people around, and a line of kids waiting for Mom to sign their books. Afterward we went out for burgers with some of Mom's friends who had come to the event. Simon wasn't there because he had stayed home with Charlie, who was just a baby, and Mom told everyone that I was her "date" for the evening. She asked me why I was being so quiet. "I'm thinking," I told her.

"About what?" Mom asked.

"Nothing," I said.

"She sounds like a teenager already, Mer," one of Mom's friends said. I was only nine, and all the grown-ups started laughing.

Even after I realized that the man at the bookstore probably wasn't my donor, I never really stopped looking for the man who was. But in all the times that I looked for him, I didn't think of him being anyone else's donor. Now it was all I could think about. It's funny how much time you have to think when you're grounded and not speaking to your family. You get home and there's nothing to do because there's no one to talk to. All those little conversations about what you did during the day or what you're going to eat for dinner never happen, and all of a sudden there is so much time on your hands. Since I wasn't talking to Mom or Simon, I had plenty of time to think about the Lyon's Sibling Registry and all the siblings I might have. Half siblings, as related to me as Charlie was. Would they look like me? More like me than Charlie does? What were their names? Where did they live? Would I like them if I met them? Would they like me?

For days my parents' credit card was practically burning a hole in my wallet. Every time I went to pull it out, I got worried about all the trouble I could get into. When Simon had handed me the card the year before, back when we lived in Maryland, he'd given me a whole lecture about being responsible and recognizing when something is an emergency. "Emergencies only," I'd told him. "I promise."

"And you know, Leah, an emergency isn't a sweater or a pair of pants that you really want," Simon had said.

"I know that," I'd said. "You act like I'm some bad kid who spends money without asking any chance I get. I never do things like that."

Simon had laughed and shaken his head. He patted my head absently, the way he did sometimes. "You're right," he said. "You're a great kid. I know you'll be responsible. If there's something you want, just call us. We'll figure it out."

But it wasn't like I could just call Mom or Simon about this one. We weren't even speaking, and I doubted that Simon still thought I was a great kid. If I used the card, it would be without their permission, and I was pretty sure they would disagree that it was an emergency. Still, I wanted to use it. Maybe they wouldn't even realize it was me. It was the same account they used, after all. Mom might think the charge came from Simon, and Simon might think the charge came from Mom. It was only $14.95. They might not even look that carefully, and chances were that they wouldn't get the bill for a long time. On Wednesday night, four days after I had first found the Lyon's Sibling Registry, I finally pulled the credit card out of my wallet. Then I sat down in front of my computer and pulled up the website for Lyon's Reproductive Services. I clicked on Lyon's Sibling Registry, and clicked on the link to register.

My heart was pounding as I entered in my information. A couple times I even mistyped because I was so nervous, and I wondered if it was a sign that I was doing something that I shouldn't. Then I felt stupid for worrying about it. I really don't think there are such things as signs. I had to come up with a log-in name and password. I didn't want to use my real name as my log-in. I had been trying hard to seem normal and keep my secret, and I wasn't sure I was ready for people to know. Even though I knew that people from school were probably not going online to the Lyon's Sibling Registry, I just didn't want to take any chances. I decided to call myself NYgirl. For my password I picked "Charlie," since he was the sibling I already knew about. I pressed enter and a screen popped up that said REGISTRANT CONSENT FORM on the top. The print was really small and I knew it was a lot of legal stuff. I started reading, but it was hard to understand. I tried not to think that it was another sign that I shouldn't register. I scrolled down to the bottom of the page, clicked the button that said "I consent" and pressed enter again. Finally the words "Thank you for registering" popped up. I think it's funny how you always get thanked whenever you spend money. I logged in with my new identity, and then there were choices. I could "post a message" or "read a message." I clicked the button to read the messages. They were organized by donor number. You could click on a number and read all the messages attached to it. I began scrolling down quickly, looking for Donor 730.

The donor numbers were in order, but I noticed that the list sometimes skipped over numbers, and I hoped I hadn't just wasted fifteen bucks and risked getting in trouble over nothing. I was getting farther down the list, Donor 655, Donor 713, Donor 725, and then finally I saw it: Donor 730. I clicked again, and four messages popped up.

I read each of them. They didn't say very much—just

names, ages, and phone numbers. I pulled out a piece of paper from my desk and folded it down the middle. Then I listed the names on the left side: Samantha, Andrew, Henry, and Tate. On the right side I wrote their ages and phone numbers.

I sat back and stared at my list. My handwriting had started to look a lot like Mom's, so it looked almost like one of her lists. Except I knew it was a list she would never make. Four names. Four siblings. Three brothers and a sister. Samantha was thirteen, just like me. Like twins, except we had different mothers. The boys were all younger. Andrew and Henry were twelve, and Tate was nine. I wondered what Charlie would think if he ever found out I had three other younger brothers. At least three other brothers—who knew how many kids came from Donor 730? As I stared at the paper, I imagined drawing my family tree now. It would be much bigger than Charlie's, with hundreds of branches for all of the siblings I might have. If we ever had a reunion, like Simon's family, we could fill a whole park with just our family. All of us, with our brown hair, olive skin, and green eyes.

I turned back to the screen and looked at the "post a message" link. If I clicked it, I would be the fifth kid to write something under Donor 730. I just couldn't do it. It was one thing to find out about having siblings. But it was another to actually admit I was one of them and to tell them my name. Then anyone with a credit card could find out about me.

I logged off the Lyon's Sibling Registry and shut down my computer. Then I folded up my list and put it away in my desk drawer. It didn't matter whether or not I was looking at it. I had already memorized it. I lay down on my bed, waiting for my heart to stop beating so fast. I knew it would be hard to fall asleep, and I wished I could just blink my eyes and have it be morning already. After years of wishing the night would last longer so I wouldn't have to wake up and go to school, I actually wanted it to be time for school. It was better than lying in my room all by myself. How could finding out I had more siblings actually make me feel lonelier? The house was so quiet. Charlie was probably already in bed. Mom and Simon might be downstairs sitting in the den, or maybe they had gone to sleep already. At least they had each other. Sometimes I wished it were still just Mom and me. Now Mom had Simon, and I was all alone. Maybe I just missed being young enough to not worry about everything. Back when I was Charlie's age, I felt like I could tell Mom everything. Now I had discovered one of the most important things about myself, and there was no one to tell.

I stared at the clock, wishing I could fast-forward it. Of course when you are waiting for it to be a certain time, the time leading up to it goes so much slower. I decided to close my eyes. In seventh grade we read a study in science class about sleep cycles. We had to keep a sleep journal. Some kids said they had a hard time falling asleep at night, and our teacher said it is better to close your eyes when you can't sleep than to lie awake with your eyes open. Something about closing your eyes fools your body into feeling like it's getting some rest. I closed my eyes and the colors behind my eyelids swirled around, blue and black. I tried to imagine what it would be like to meet Samantha or Andrew or Henry or Tate. Would it be like finding a long-lost loved one? Would it be horribly awkward? Would we all be disappointed? What does it mean to be related to someone, anyway? Just because we share some DNA doesn't mean we would like one another. The thing about siblings is, usually you grow up together, so you have to love each other. I didn't really have a choice about loving Charlie. Mom came home from the hospital one day when I was eight years old, and this little red-faced baby was with her. One of his first words was "We-ah," which is what he called me until he was three. I tried to make up bedtime stories for him, just like Mom did for me, so I invented Super Charlie. Mom and Simon used to get annoyed because I was supposed to be calming Charlie down and getting him ready for bed, but Super Charlie liked to jump on the bed and pretend he was flying. "Here he comes to save the day!" I would shout.

I didn't ever have to think about what to say to Charlie. He was just there. But that would be different with my other siblings, and I had no idea what I would say.

I opened my eyes to see just how late it was. The clock across from my bed said 1:14. I know it sounds kind of lame, but I don't think I had ever been awake that late before on a school night. There is something sort of eerie about being the only person awake in the middle of the night. I began to hear the house creaking. When everything else is so quiet, a little creak can sound really loud. I pulled my pillow over my head to drown out the sounds. But even with the pillow over my head I could still hear something. It started out like a kind of moan, and I wondered if it was just the wind. Then it got louder. I felt my heart start to race all over again. I pulled the pillow off my head and I lay perfectly still and listened. It sounded more like an animal than the wind. I heard someone call out "Mommy!" and I realized it was just Charlie.

"Mommy! Daddy!" he called. I waited to hear Mom or Simon running down the hall, but the only sound was Charlie. Maybe they couldn't hear him because their room is too far away. They should have installed that monitor they had when he was a baby, back in the pink house when all the rooms were on top of one another and they didn't really need it to hear him. Now we were in a bigger house. Charlie and I had rooms right next to each other, but Mom and Simon's room was all the way down at the end of the hall. We could really have used that monitor now. Charlie kept crying. I heard his cries get loud and then go soft as he gathered his breath, and then get loud again, like an ocean that ebbs and flows. I pulled the pillow over my head again. It muffled the sound, but didn't drown it out completely. Any second they would hear him, or he would go running down the hall to their room. Any second he would get tired and stop crying. From under the pillow I heard him call out, "Leah!" Because he was crying, it came out like "We-ah," just like when he was a baby. I swung my legs out of bed and headed to Charlie.

I flicked on the light switch by Charlie's door, and we both squinted from it being suddenly bright. Charlie was panting from crying so hard. His face was as red as a tomato, and his hair was flattened down onto his head from sweating. "Leah." He gulped. "I thought everyone was gone. I thought you'd all left me alone."

"Oh, Charlie," I said. "We wouldn't ever leave without you."

"What if the house was burning down and you had to leave really fast?" he asked.

"Then I would come in here and scoop you up and take you outside with me," I told him. I went to sit down on the bed with him. He climbed into my arms, all sticky and wet. At first I thought it was just sweat, but then I realized he'd also wet the bed. "Did you have an accident?" I asked him.

"I didn't think anyone was here!" he wailed. "It's not my fault. I thought you'd gone and I was all alone."

Like I could have gone anywhere. I was grounded, after all. But I knew exactly what he meant about feeling all alone. "It's okay," I told him. "I'll go get Mom."

"No, no," Charlie sobbed. "Don't leave me." He clung to me. I didn't push him off right away even though he was all wet and it was starting to smell. I rested my chin on his sweaty head and waited until his breaths had slowed and they were almost normal. How could I ever love any other siblings as much as I loved Charlie? He twisted in my arms and I thought maybe he was ready for me to leave him.

"Charlie?" I said.

"Yeah?"

"Can you count to twenty?"

"Yeah," Charlie said.

"Okay, start counting," I said. It was a trick Mom used to use on me when I woke up sick. I would want her to stay with me, and she would tell me to count while she went to get medicine. "I'll be back before you get to twenty," I told Charlie. "I'm just going to get Mom."

I ran down the hall. It was dark except for the thin line of light coming from Charlie's room. I thought I could hear him counting, but maybe it was just in my head. I pushed open the door to Mom and Simon's room and went over to Mom's side of the bed. "Mom," I said. "Mom, wake up."

"What is it?" she asked.

"Charlie's crying," I said. "He wet the bed."

Mom jumped out of bed as if she'd been awake all along. She always moved fast when Charlie needed her. She took off down the hall, and I walked behind her. I got to his door but I didn't go in again. Mom was with him, pulling his shirt over his head. I heard Charlie say, "You weren't there, and Daddy wasn't there."

"I know," Mom said. "I'm sorry."

"But then Leah was there," Charlie said. He looked up and saw me in the doorway. "You got me," he said.

"Yeah," I said.

Mom turned around. "Thanks, Leah," she said. She didn't even correct me and say "*yes*" like she usually does when I say "yeah." Then she turned back to finish cleaning Charlie up.

chapterseven

I had been grounded for almost a whole week. Even though I was sort of back on speaking terms with Mom and Simon, they hadn't said anything about my grounding being over. On my way to pick up Charlie from school on Friday, I called Mom to see if I could take him for ice cream, and she said yes. I guess having Charlie out of the house so she could keep writing mattered more than punishing me. I didn't tell her that Avery and Callie would be there too. If Charlie told her, I decided I could make it sound like it was just a coincidence that we had bumped into them, and then it would have been rude not to hang out with them. After all, it wasn't their fault that my parents were insanely strict and spiteful.

Avery and Callie had gone straight to the ice-cream parlor after school instead of coming with me to pick up Charlie. It's this little old-fashioned place on the main street in town. It gets kind of crowded when school lets out, so it was better for them to go early and save a table. Avery wanted to make sure we had a table in the back because those are the ones with the mini-jukeboxes, and besides, I didn't want Charlie to blab that Avery and Callie had come with me to pick him up. Then Mom would know for sure that it wasn't just a coincidence that we ran into them. I ran over to Charlie's school and got there in time to see him shake Mrs. Trager's hand. He shaded his eyes with his other hand, and when he spotted me, he bounded over toward me.

Charlie handed me something made out of pipe cleaners and construction paper. It looked like a crumpled mess even though he said it was a caterpillar. "Cool," I said. Charlie sighed. "What's the matter?" I asked.

"Fridays are my worst days," he told me. He hunched his shoulders over and looked suddenly old.

"How come?" I asked.

"No school for two days," he said.

Isn't it funny how the worst thing for one person can be the best thing for another? It made me feel grown-up. "Would it make you feel better if I told you we were getting ice cream?" I asked him.

"Oh, yeah," Charlie said.

"Come on," I told him. I pulled him along a little faster. Charlie is a really slow walker.

It felt strange to be back out in the world after being grounded. I imagined it was sort of like the feeling a prisoner gets when he's let out of jail. Maybe being grounded wasn't quite that bad, but for the past few days I hadn't gone anywhere except to school and back home. The air was cooler now than it had been a week ago. Indian summer was ending. The leaves were already starting to change colors. They weren't falling off the trees yet, but if you looked closely, you could see the edges starting to turn, from green to yellow.

Back in Maryland, when I was little, Mom used to help me collect leaves when they fell off the trees. We pressed them between phone books to make them really flat, and then I'd glue them onto construction paper and make collages.

Charlie stopped and bent down to retie a shoelace that had come undone. He mumbled to himself as he tied: "Two loops, put one under, and pull." I breathed in deeply. I know it sounds dumb, but after being cooped up at home for a week, the air seemed so much fresher.

A couple minutes later we rounded the corner of Riverdale Avenue. Once the ice-cream parlor was in sight, Charlie started walking so fast that he was pulling me. We walked in and I spotted Avery and Callie sitting at the back. "Hey, look," I said to Charlie. "Avery's here."

"Where?" he asked. I bent down to him and pointed to the back table. "I like Avery," Charlie announced. "Every time I see her I get to eat dessert!"

I wanted to say hello to Avery and Callie, but Charlie couldn't wait to get his ice cream. I gave him money to order for both of us and went over to the table in the back. Charlie likes to order by himself, but I didn't let him out of my sight. His head was barely higher than the counter. I watched the guy behind the counter hand Charlie his change, and then Charlie headed over to us. He walked extra slowly because he was carrying ice cream for both him and me—a scoop of chocolate in a cone with rainbow sprinkles for himself, and a plain scoop of chocolate in a cup for me. I don't really like cones. They're okay in the beginning, but I like to eat my ice cream slowly, so that it gets kind of soupy, and the cone gets too soggy and messy that way. I stood up to help Charlie, and Avery got up and sat in the booth next to Callie so that Charlie could sit next to me.

"Oooh, it's a music box," he said.

"A jukebox," I corrected him.

"Here," Avery said, fishing a quarter out of her pocket. "Why don't you pick a song?"

"Cool," Charlie said. "Hey, Leah, what's that song Daddy always sings that Mommy doesn't like?"

"'You Give Love a Bad Name,'" I told him.

"Yeah, that's it," he said. "I love that song."

"Bon Jovi," Avery said. "That's very old school. Awesome choice. How come your mom doesn't like it?"

"She doesn't like that Charlie points his fingers like a gun whenever he sings about being shot through the heart," I told her.

"Help me find it, Leah," Charlie said.

"What do you say?" I asked, the way Mom sometimes does.

"Please," Charlie said automatically. I reached over him and turned the dials on the jukebox.

"They might not have it," I warned him. Charlie clasped his hands together like he was praying. I heard him mutter "please, please" to himself. "You're in luck," I said after a few seconds. "Here it is." Charlie dropped the quarter in, and I showed him what button to press.

"How come it's not coming on?" Charlie asked.

"You have to wait," Avery explained. "All the little juke-boxes are hooked up to the same system, so you pay for a song, and then when it's your turn, it will come out of the big jukebox in the front and everyone will hear it."

"How long will it take?" he asked.

Avery shrugged. "It depends on how many people bought songs before you did."

"What if we have to leave before it comes on?" Charlie asked.

Charlie has a habit of sometimes asking too many questions. I hoped Avery and Callie didn't think he was being too annoying. I was still the new kid in school. They could still decide not to be my friends, so I wanted Charlie to act as adorable as possible. "Finish your ice cream," I told Charlie. "It will come on soon." I stirred the ice cream in my cup to make it more soupy and hoped Charlie would be quiet for at least a few minutes.

"Hey, did you guys hear from Brenna last night?" Callie asked.

"Who's Brenna?" Charlie asked. His mouth was full of ice cream so it came out kind of muffled, but I knew what he was saying.

"She's another friend of ours," I said. "She's on a trip with her parents." Brenna's father had had a business trip to New Mexico, which is where her mother's aunt lived. The aunt was really old. Brenna had never met her, and Brenna's mom decided it was a good time to take Brenna to visit her, in case she died before they got another chance to see her. So Brenna got to miss school, even though it was just the second week. Our English teacher said she should keep a journal about the trip. Brenna had shrugged. She didn't really want to go to New Mexico to meet some ancient aunt she had barely ever heard of before.

"She called me last night," Avery said. "But Chase was on the phone with Lizzie all night, and he didn't give me the message until this morning. They had a fight and then they were making up. I can't wait until he goes to college and I don't have to share the phone line with him anymore. Anyway, I was going to call Brenna back this morning, before school, but my mom said I couldn't because of the time change. It's, like, two hours earlier there."

"Where?" Charlie asked. He had swallowed so it was easier to understand him.

"In New Mexico," Avery said.

"I know Mexico," he said.

"No, not Mexico," I said. "*New* Mexico. It's another state."

"New York is a state," he said. I nodded. "And Maryland is a state too," he continued. "I've lived in two states."

Charlie hadn't managed to stay quiet for very long, but Avery just smiled. "I've only lived in one state," she told him.

I looked across the table at Callie. "She didn't call me," I said to change the subject.

"Leah's not allowed to talk on the phone," Charlie said. I shoved him a little, but not so hard that it would hurt. Apparently he thought this was funny because he smiled and kept talking. "She's in trouble because she stayed out too late. And she's not allowed to watch TV, so I get to pick every time!"

I felt myself start to blush. I hadn't really told Avery and Callie about being grounded. I didn't want them to think I was a baby. I had just pretended to be extra busy over the last few days so they wouldn't think it was strange that I didn't want to hang out after school and couldn't talk on the phone. "Anyway," I said extra loudly, so Charlie would know to shut up. "Did you hear from her?"

Callie nodded.

"Is she miserable?" Avery asked. "I'd hate it if my parents made me go across the country with them to meet some old relative I'd never heard of. It sounds even more boring than school."

"And she doesn't get to eat ice cream with us," Charlie said. Sometimes I'm impressed by how easily he can follow grown-up conversations. He's only five, after all. Mom and Simon think he's some kind of genius. They had his IQ tested right before we moved to Riverdale, and it turns out that Charlie has the highest IQ of all of us, even though he's the youngest. Sometimes I wish he weren't quite so smart, because then he'd probably be more quiet. I've never told anyone that, though. They'd probably just think I was jealous.

"She wouldn't have come here with us even if she was in Riverdale," Avery said.

"How come?" I asked.

"She and her mom are on this total health kick. Her mom lost, like, a hundred pounds last year."

"Seriously?" I asked.

"Yeah, really," Avery said. "Now Brenna never eats dessert or anything. Haven't you noticed how she is at lunch? How she only eats things on whole grain bread and always asks for extra vegetables? I don't know how she does it. I'd never be able to skip dessert all the time, and I don't think food should be such a big deal. I mean, isn't the point to enjoy it?"

"Well, just so you know, she's at least enjoying New Mexico," Callie said.

"You're kidding," Avery said.

"No, I mean it," Callie said. "She said her great-aunt is really amazing. She taught Brenna how to read palms and tell the future."

"No way!" Avery said.

"I swear," Callie told us. "Her great-aunt is passing down her calling, or something like that. Anyway, I totally know how to do it now."

"Right," Avery said. "You're not the one in New Mexico with a medium for an aunt."

"She's not a medium," Callie said. "She's a fortune-teller."

"Same difference," Avery said.

"No, there is a difference," Callie insisted. "A medium can talk to the dead." I shuddered when she said that and looked over at Charlie to make sure he was okay. He has a thing about ghosts. But he didn't seem upset about it. He was down to the end of his ice-cream cone, sticking his tongue into the last little crevice to try to lick the rest of the ice cream out. "Brenna told me everything about palm reading over the phone," Callie continued.

"You can't just learn in one phone call," Avery told her.

"Well, she told me about it, and then I looked it up on the Internet, so I really know how to do it. Give me your palm."

"No way. I'm not giving you my palm."

"Oh, come on. If you don't believe me, then what are you scared about?"

"I'm not scared," Avery said defiantly. She narrowed her eyes at Callie. I think she was waiting for Callie to admit she didn't know what she was talking about, but Callie just stared back at Avery, waiting. "Fine," Avery said, and stuck out her hand.

Callie pulled Avery's hand closer to her. "You know," Callie began, "a life line doesn't only show how long you're gonna live—it also shows you how good your life is gonna be."

"Which line is the life line?" Avery asked.

"This one," Callie said, tracing the line that started between Avery's thumb and index finger and curved down to the base of her palm. "Yours isn't solid, but that's not necessarily a bad thing. See, it has branches. Sometimes branches can mean fortune."

"Fortune is good," Avery said.

"Uh-huh," Callie said. Her shoulders were hunched and she was squinting her eyes, concentrating. "There are other lines too. Like, here's your love line. It's really strong."

"It can't be that strong," Avery said. "I haven't even been in love yet."

"Well, maybe you will be this year," Callie said. "It's totally solid, no breaks at all. But your mount of Jupiter is sort of weak."

"What does that mean?" Avery asked.

"It means you don't have confidence," Callie said.

"I have confidence," Avery insisted.

"Well, maybe there's something in particular that you're not confident about," Callie said. "But you have other lines that are really strong, even stronger than your love line, like this one. I can't remember for sure what it's called. I think it's the family line. Anyway, that one is really strong on your hand. I think it means you have a big family and everyone is really loyal."

I turned my hand over in my lap and looked down. Callie and Avery were both bent over Avery's hand, and Charlie was watching them intently, so they probably didn't notice me. The lines on my hand all seemed broken and faint. My family line was probably nonexistent. I balled my hands into fists and pressed them into my lap. Callie was finishing up with Avery. I heard Charlie beside me. "My turn, my turn," he said.

"All right, Charlie," Callie said. He sat up on his knees and placed his hand on the table, palm up. Callie told him his lines were all strong. "This must be the best palm in the world," she told him.

"What about my Jupiter line?" Charlie asked. He sounded worried, I guess because of what Callie had said about Avery.

"Oh, your mount of Jupiter is just fine. I can tell you have a lot of confidence," Callie told him. I knew she was just saying it because he was young and she wanted to be nice, but Charlie totally believed her. Avery rolled her eyes, but Charlie didn't see her.

"Did you hear that, Leah?" he said excitedly. I nodded. "Now it's your turn," Charlie said.

"That's okay," I said.

"Come on," Callie said.

"Yeah," Avery said. "Even I did it."

"Even I did it," Charlie echoed. They were all looking at me, waiting for me to give in. My hands were still curled into fists, and all of a sudden they seemed to be sweating hard. I could feel the moisture between my fingers. I didn't want Callie examining my family line, but I couldn't say that out loud. And I couldn't think of another excuse not to have my palm read. "Come on, Leah," Charlie said. He reached under the table and tugged at my wrist.

"Fine," I said. I uncurled my palm and wiped it on my jeans and let Charlie pull my hand onto the table. But then I heard Bon Jovi begin to sing. "Charlie," I said, "your song." He forgot all about my palm.

"It's finally playing!" he said. He stood up on his knees and put his hands together like a gun.

"Don't point the gun at Avery," I told him. I knew I sounded like my mom.

Charlie made a fist and brought it to his mouth like a microphone. "You give love a bad name," he sang. He turned to me. "I want to go see the big jukebox," he said. I turned toward the front of the restaurant. It was much more crowded than it had been when we first arrived.

"You can't go alone," I told him.

"Will you take me?" he asked. "Please, please, please?"

"Uh-huh," I said, nodding. I would have done anything to avoid having my palm read, and I started to get up.

"Oh, look," Callie said. "That guy Ian from my math class is over at the jukebox." Avery and I looked over to where Callie was pointing. I recognized the skinny kid with dark hair that Callie sometimes stares at when we're in the cafeteria.

"His brother works here," Avery said.

"How do you know?" Callie asked.

"Chase knows him," Avery said. "They're both seniors."

"Oh," Callie said. "Well, I should go ask Ian what the math homework is this weekend. I didn't write it down."

"Of course you didn't," Avery said.

Callie ignored her. "I'll take Charlie," she said. She stood up and took Charlie's hand. I watched them walk over to the jukebox. Callie lifted Charlie so he could see better.

"Can you believe Callie?" Avery said, and I snapped my head back to face her. "She's nuts, using Charlie just to be able to stand next to Ian Michaelson. And I bet there's no such thing as a Jupiter mount or a family line."

I shrugged. "Sorry about my brother," I told her.

"What do you mean?" she asked.

"If you thought he was being annoying," I said.

"You shouldn't worry so much about what other people think," Avery said. She always said that. It was easy for her to say, since she was the kind of person people tried to be like, but it would be impossible for me to act like I didn't care what other people thought of me. I shrugged again. "What's with you today?" Avery asked.

"What do you mean?" I asked.

"You seem upset about something," she said. "Is it about being grounded?"

"No," I said.

"You can tell me, you know," Avery said.

"No," I said. Avery looked at me funny. "I mean, it's all right. I'm okay," I said.

Charlie came running back to the table a few minutes later. "It's so cool," he said about the jukebox. "I wish I could have one."

Callie came up behind him. "Did you find out about your math homework?" Avery asked her.

"Yeah," Callie said. "You know, Ian said his brother said they're looking for people to work here after school. Maybe I should apply."

"Oh, please," Avery said. "You just want to work here so you could see Ian more."

"No," Callie said. "I just think it would be good to make money."

"If you worked here, would you give us ice cream whenever we wanted?" Charlie asked.

"Of course," Callie said.

"Cool," Charlie said.

"Well, we should probably get going," I said. "My mom doesn't like it if I keep Charlie out too late. Come on, Char."

"You sure?" Avery said. I nodded. Avery held out her hand to Charlie. "Aren't you going to shake my hand good-bye?"

"No," Charlie said. "You're not a teacher." He climbed up onto the booth and hugged Avery good-bye.

"Call me tonight if you want to talk," Avery said.

"I will," I told her, even though I wasn't actually allowed to use the phone, and even if I were, I wouldn't call her anyway. I didn't think she would understand anything about it. Her family wasn't anything like mine. It was solid and strong. She knew exactly who her father was. She didn't get grounded for no good reason, and she didn't have half siblings scattered around the country. There were some things I couldn't tell anyone else. Except maybe a sibling. Like Samantha. I had her phone number in my desk at home. Technically I wasn't allowed to use the phone since I was grounded, but I could tell Mom it was for school. I could say I was doing a project with a girl named Samantha and ask for special permission to use the phone. I knew she wouldn't say no if she thought it was for school. Suddenly I was in a hurry. "Come on, Charlie," I said.

It took a while to walk home because Charlie is so slow. Mom met us at the door and told us that she had ordered in again. "Will you be eating with us this time?" she asked me. I hadn't sat at the table with Mom and Simon all week since I was so mad at them.

"I don't know," I said. "I have this project for English. The teacher broke us up into pairs and I'm supposed to work on it with this girl Samantha. I thought I might get started on it. Can I use the phone if it's for school?"

"Yes," Mom said.

"Thanks," I said. I started to go upstairs.

"Leah," Mom called, and I turned back to look at her. "I think you've learned your lesson, don't you?" I nodded. "That's what I thought," Mom said. "I think you've been grounded long enough. Thanks for helping with Charlie."

"No problem," I said, and I headed the rest of the way up the stairs.

chaptereight

I knew calling Samantha was a long distance phone call because I had to dial a different area code. I was pretty sure that meant the call was more expensive, and I decided not to think about what Mom and Simon would do when they got the phone bill. I just picked up the phone.

I tried calling Samantha twice on Friday night and again on Saturday, but I didn't get to speak to her until Sunday. By then I had memorized her phone number, and I was used to the way the answering machine at her house sounded when it picked up on the other end. It was a woman's voice: "You have reached the Holland residence. Please leave a message for Anna or Samantha at the tone." My hands had been pretty sweaty the first few times I called, but by Sunday I was starting to expect that no one would be home. I was lying on my bed counting the rings. The answering machine always picked up after four rings. But this time, halfway through the second ring, a woman said "Hello?" I clutched the phone with both hands and sat up. "Hello?" the woman said again.

"Um, is Samantha there?" I asked. I knew my voice sounded strange, not at all like my regular voice, but since the woman had never heard my regular voice before, she couldn't tell that it was coming out differently.

"Just a sec," the woman said. I recognized her voice from the answering machine. She was probably Anna. Anna, who had gone to Lyon's Reproductive Services and picked out Donor 730, just like my mom had. I wondered what she looked like. Sometimes you can get an idea of what someone looks like by the way they sound, but I couldn't picture Anna at all in my head. I heard muffled voices through the phone, and then footsteps. My hands had started sweating again. I could feel the phone getting slippery.

"Hello?" a voice said. It was a younger voice this time, like around my age.

"Is this Samantha?" I asked.

"Yeah. Who's this?"

"My name is Leah," I said. "I got your number off the Lyon's Sibling Registry."

"Oh my God!" Samantha said. Her voice let out a kind of squeal. Then we both started laughing. It was the nervous kind of laughter—the sound that you make when you don't know what else to do. After a few seconds Samantha said, "I can't believe you're a girl. I mean, so far I've only heard from boys."

"Oh," I said. I knew I sounded dumb, but I wasn't sure what to say.

"I mean, you're calling about Donor 730, right?" Samantha asked. I started to answer but Samantha kept talking. "Oh, God, I hope you are. If you're not I'll be so embarrassed!"

"No, no," I told Samantha. "I'm calling about Donor 730. He's my donor too."

"Thank God!" Samantha said. She said "God" a lot. It wasn't exactly a word that came up a whole lot in my house. Mom says she's not sure if she even believes in God. Simon does, but he doesn't make a big deal about it. Samantha wasn't really using the word "God" in any religious way. I giggled again, nervously. I wasn't sure what to say. "How old are you?" Samantha asked.

"Thirteen," I told her.

"So am I," she said.

"I know," I said.

"Right. This is crazy, isn't it?" Samantha said.

"It sure is," I said. "I only found out about the Lyon's Sibling Registry a week ago."

"Oh," she said. "I've been on it about nine months. I've talked to the other kids from Donor 730—Andrew, Henry, and Tate. That's why I was so happy you were a girl."

"I saw their names," I said. "I called you first because you were the only girl."

"Crazy," she said again. "A sister. I always wanted a sister. When I found out about the registry, the thing I was most excited about was finding a sister, but for the last nine months I've only known about three brothers." When she said that word, "brothers," I thought of Charlie downstairs, watching his *Lion King* DVD on the big television in the den. I thought of the way he mouths the words as he watches the movie; he's seen it so many times that he knows it by heart. "Don't get me wrong," Samantha continued. "The boys are cool. You'll really like them."

"I have another brother," I told Samantha. "You know,

besides you guys on the Lyon's Sibling Registry. His name is Charlie. He's five."

"Another brother," Samantha said. The way she said it made me realize she considered Charlie another newfound sibling of her own. "So your mom bought more vials?"

"What do you mean?" I asked.

"You know," she said. "More vials of Donor 730. Some people buy more vials so if they have another baby later on, the kids will be related."

"Did your mom buy more vials?" I asked.

"Yeah," Samantha said. "She's got extra vials in the freezer. It's sort of gross. But I guess it's a good thing. There's a woman my mother heard of whose daughter had leukemia or something. The daughter needed a bone marrow transplant and it's best to get a transplant from a relative because your blood is the same that way. The woman had more vials from the donor, so she had another baby to help her daughter. But if you already have a brother, your mom wouldn't need to have another baby."

"Charlie's my stepfather's son," I told her. "I guess technically he's only my half brother. But I always call him my brother."

"What's he like?" she asked.

"Who? My stepfather?" I said.

"No, Charlie," Samantha said.

"I guess he's like other five-year-olds," I told her. "He's okay most of the time. He likes *The Lion King* and Bon Jovi."

"Are you guys really close?" Samantha asked.

"Yeah," I said. Then I corrected myself automatically, "I mean, *yes.* We're close. He's only five, so there's a lot I can't say to him. But I love him a lot. I can't imagine not having him."

"That's good," Samantha said. "I always thought it would be hard if my mom married someone and had a baby—you know, because it would be their kid *together*."

"I guess it's hard sometimes," I admitted, remembering Simon's family reunion where they all loved Charlie best.

"I figured," Samantha said. "That's too bad." Her voice was softer and I thought maybe she felt sorry for me. I thought about telling her most of the time it wasn't so bad. Simon adopted me, and he treated me just like a daughter. He even punished me just like I was his real kid. Most of the time I loved him like he was my dad. I remembered his face when I told him he wasn't my dad. It was all so complicated and I felt strange talking to Samantha about private things. She might be my half sister, at least biologically, but she was also a stranger.

"What's your mom like?" I asked Samantha to change the subject.

"She's cool," Samantha said. She told me her mother is sort of older. She had Samantha when she was forty years old. They live in Pennsylvania, in a town called Haverford. There's a college in Haverford—actually called Haverford—where her mom works. Her mom's a guidance counselor and helps kids when they're depressed. Samantha told me that most college students get depressed right before they graduate, when they're scared about being in the real world and not being with their friends every day anymore. It reminded me of how Avery said Chase got upset about being away from Lizzie. "So my mom helps them figure out what they should be doing, and how to channel their energy into positive things, and all that," Samantha said. It sounded sort of similar to my mom's job, except my mom doesn't have office hours and meet with students one-on-one. She just writes books to try to help kids.

"Does your mom want you to go to Haverford?" I asked.

"She knows I won't, so she doesn't try to talk me into it, thank God," Samantha said. "I can't wait to go to college. I know it's not happening for a few years, but I think it'll be really cool to go. My mom always says it's the best years of your life. I think she just says that because I complain about school now, and she wants me to look forward to college. I think I'd like to go somewhere like California. It'd be great to be so close to the beach, don't you think?"

"I don't know if I want to go that far away," I said. "I mean, Charlie will only be ten when I go to college."

"It must be nice to have a sibling like that," Samantha said. "Not off some registry, but one you've grown up with. Even if it is a half sibling."

"It is," I said. I heard Samantha sigh sort of wistfully on the other end of the phone, and I realized that I had stopped feeling as though I were talking to a stranger. Maybe it was because Samantha was so talkative. She was probably one of those people who wasn't shy around anyone, like Avery. Still, I was starting to feel more comfortable. "It doesn't mean you can't be close with siblings you meet through the registry," I told her.

"I know," she said. "Hey, do you ever worry that one day you'll meet some guy and fall in love, and then it will turn out that his father was also Donor 730?"

"I never thought of that before," I said.

"It just occurred to me," Samantha said. "But that would really be awful. I mean, it's totally possible."

"I guess it's possible," I said.

"I think it would make a good movie. You know, like one of those made-for-television movies on the Lifetime channel. My mom and I watch them sometimes. Maybe I should write a script."

"It would be perfect if you wrote a script and then went to college in California. They make all the movies out there," I said.

"Totally," Samantha said, sounding like a Valley girl. "Hollywood, here I come!"

We talked for a few more minutes. Samantha gave me her e-mail address and asked me to send her a picture. She asked for my e-mail address so she could do the same. Then I heard the phone click, and Simon's voice. "Hello? Hello?"

"Simon," I said. "I'm on the phone."

"Oh, Leah, honey," he said. "I'm sorry, but I just got an e-mail and I need to call someone for work. My cell phone doesn't get great service in the house."

"I'll get off in two minutes," I told him.

"Thanks," he said. The phone clicked again as he hung up.

"That was my stepfather," I said. "I guess I better go."

"Wait a sec," Samantha said. "Can I have your phone number first?"

"Of course," I said. I gave her my cell phone number. I didn't want to give her the house phone number in case Mom or Simon answered. Samantha said she would call me. I knew she meant it, and I was glad. I stood up from my bed and headed downstairs. I could hear Mom shuffling around in the kitchen and I thought about the donor vials in Samantha's freezer. I walked in. Mom looked surprised to see me, as if she'd forgotten all about me until I walked into the kitchen.

"Leah!" she said. "Are you having dinner with us?"

"It depends on what you're making," I said. That was a joke from when I was little. I used to never feel hungry until I found out that Mom was making something I liked to eat.

"Spaghetti and meatballs," Mom said. "Charlie's request."

"I guess I'll eat with you, then," I said.

"Good," Mom said. "You can help with the salad." She handed me a head of lettuce to wash. "So who were you talking to?" she asked.

"When?" I asked.

"Just now," Mom said. "Simon said you were on the phone."

"Just someone from school," I said.

"About your project?" she asked.

"Yes." I started tearing pieces of lettuce to put into a bowl. "Mom?" I said. She looked up from the cutting board, where she was dicing tomatoes. "Do you have extra vials from Lyon's?" I asked.

"What are you talking about?" she asked.

"Do you have extra, you know, from when you went there to have me?" I said.

"Why are you asking me?"

"I don't know," I said. "I'm just curious."

"I did at the time," Mom said. "I don't anymore. I married Simon, and we had Charlie."

"So you threw them away?" I asked incredulously.

"Yes," Mom said simply.

"I can't believe you," I said.

"What do you mean?" Mom asked.

"Well, what if I needed a heart or a lung transplant, and the only hope was having a whole, real sibling to be the donor, and you threw that chance away?"

"I don't think they perform heart or lung transplants from living donors," Mom said.

"Well, bone marrow, then," I said. "What if I had leukemia and I needed a bone marrow transplant?"

"I don't like this conversation," Mom said. "It's too morbid."

"No, really," I said. "What if I needed a transplant?"

"Plenty of people are only children, Leah," Mom said impatiently. "It's not that unusual. You could get a transplant from a stranger who just happens to match your blood type. Or maybe I would match. Maybe Charlie would match."

"Maybe you and Charlie wouldn't match," I said.

"Maybe," Mom said.

"Parents don't think about how the things they decide affect their kids' lives forever," I said.

"Of course I think about you," Mom said.

"Whatever," I said, which is one of the words on Mom's list of words she hates. It's not that it's grammatically incorrect, she just thinks it's obnoxious.

"Leah," Mom said, shaking her head. "There are no guarantees that you would match with someone who was your 'whole' sibling anyway."

"But the chances would be better if it wasn't just a half sibling," I said.

"Yes," Mom said. "Okay. You're right. Can we end this conversation now?"

"Fine," I said.

"Bring the garlic bread to the table," Mom said.

Suddenly I felt like an outsider again, and I wasn't sure I still wanted to have dinner with all of them. I picked up the plate of bread and walked out to the table, thinking that maybe I would just leave it there and continue going up the stairs to my room. "Hey, Leah," Charlie called. I looked up, and he was sitting in my seat.

"That's my chair," I said.

"We traded," Charlie said.

"You can't do that," I told him. "You can only trade with someone if they agree to a trade."

"But you weren't eating with us, and I like this seat better," Charlie said.

Mom came up behind me. "Let him have the seat," she said. "He likes to be able to see the television from the table."

"You never let *me* watch television at dinner," I said. Mom had made a really big deal about dinner when I was younger. It was the time she would ask me about school and tell me about what she was writing. Sometimes she let me play music in the background, but I was never allowed to watch television.

"I guess I've learned to pick my battles in my old age," Mom said.

"That's not fair," I said, even though Mom hates when I say that. She says life isn't fair in general. There are a lot of people out there who are much worse off, and we have to be grateful for what we have and work with what we've got. I hate when she gets all philosophical about life being unfair. It's just a way for her to avoid the fact that she's being nicer to Charlie than she is to me.

"Oh, Leah—," Mom started.

"Forget it," I said, cutting her off. "I'm not hungry anyway."

"I really wish you would sit with us," Mom said. "You know how I feel about family dinners."

"Right," I said. "That's why you're letting Charlie watch TV."

"But it's my favorite show," Charlie said. He sounded scared, and Mom put down the plate she was carrying and patted his shoulder.

I rolled my eyes. "Here," I said, thrusting the garlic bread at Mom. I headed up to my room even though I really was hungry. My stomach was even growling a little.

Later that night I lay in bed thinking about everything. It was late and the house was still. I hated fighting with my family. I wished Charlie would wake up again. It's not like I wanted him to have a bad dream or anything, I just didn't

want to feel lonely anymore. But kids forget things so easily. I hadn't slept well in over a week, and Charlie didn't
have any trouble sleeping anymore, just like nothing had
ever happened to wake him up and make him feel scared. I
turned over in my bed and stared at the phone on my desk.
If it weren't so late, maybe I would have called Samantha
again. I couldn't think of anything else to do, and there were
so many things to ask her—thirteen years to catch up on.
I said her name out loud, "Samantha Holland." It echoed
over and over again in my head. She was my sister, and I
didn't even know her middle name. I didn't know if she
even had one. Some people don't. Maybe her mom thought
middle names were silly. You never really use them anyway.
Or maybe she was named after someone, just like I was,
so her middle name was important. I wanted to find out.
Sometimes I think of things at night and in the morning I
can't remember what they were. I rolled out of bed and sat
down at my desk to write a list of questions for Samantha,
so I wouldn't forget what I wanted to ask her.

chapternine

All of a sudden it was October. I wasn't grounded anymore, but I still felt different, like all the things that had happened to me had turned me into a different person. Things with my parents were still strange. I looked the same as before, but sometimes I caught them looking at me funny, like they didn't quite recognize me anymore. I wondered how they could tell what I'd been doing, and I worried about what would happen when the credit card bill came and Lyon's Sibling Registry was on the statement.

But mostly things were crazy at our house because Mom's book deadline was getting closer and closer. "This month is so short!" she said to me one day. I had just come home from school with Charlie. He said he was hungry, and even though it was barely four o'clock, I was getting hungry too. I hadn't eaten much all day. Avery and Callie had had some special meal with their Spanish class, so it was just Brenna and me at lunch. Brenna had brought some tofu and brown rice concoction that she wanted me to share, but it tasted strange. I didn't want to hurt Brenna's feelings, so I pushed it around on my plate and tried to make it look like I was eating it. I went in to ask Mom what time Simon would be home and if we could eat dinner early.

"What do you mean, the month is so short?" I asked her. "It's thirty-one days—that's the longest a month can be."

"February is the shortest month," Charlie said from behind me. "Sometimes it's twenty-eight days and sometimes it's twenty-nine days, but it's always the shortest."

"This month *feels* like the shortest," Mom said. "It feels even shorter than February."

That night at dinner Mom said she needed us all out of the house as much as possible, even on the weekends, because having us around made it harder for her to work.

"What if we stay home and don't bother you?" Charlie asked.

"Even if you guys were hanging out in another part of the house and didn't talk to me at all, it would distract me," Mom told him. I knew what she meant. Whenever I'm working on something I don't want to do, I'll make excuses not to do it. Like when I had to study for my math quiz, I kept asking Charlie if he wanted to play Monopoly. "I only have this one little month left," Mom said. "If you're here, I'll want to be with you instead of writing." Simon offered to take Charlie and me into Manhattan on Saturday to show us his new office. Charlie loves offices because he gets to make copies of his hands and arms on the Xerox machines. The last time we went to Simon's office, back when we helped Simon clean out his old office in Baltimore, Charlie wanted to make a Xerox copy of his face. I thought it would be kind of cool to see, but Simon said no. The Xerox machine had a really bright light that flashed whenever a copy was made, and Simon was afraid it would hurt Charlie's eyes.

I used to like going to Simon's office too, but suddenly it seemed boring. I really didn't want to help Charlie make Xerox copies of his hands, or smile and shake hands with anyone who happened to be in Simon's office on a Saturday.

"I'm not really in the mood to go to Manhattan," I told Simon. "Besides, I have plans already." The part about having plans was true. Avery had invited me to go apple picking with her and Chase. Apparently Chase and Lizzie had made a tradition of going apple picking every fall, but Chase and Lizzie were fighting again so Chase was taking Avery this year. "That way he can pick apples and think about Lizzie and be miserable, instead of sitting at home and thinking about Lizzie and being miserable," Avery had explained. "You have to come with me, or else I'll be alone with my miserable brother all day." I knew from the way she said it that she was actually glad that Chase had invited her, but I still wanted to go.

"What kind of plans?" Simon asked.

"Avery asked me if I wanted to go apple picking with her and Chase on Saturday," I said. "They're going to this orchard upstate. I could bring a bunch of apples home with me."

"You sure you don't want to come to the office?" Simon asked. "I'd love to show you and Chuck around, and we could go to Serendipity for lunch. They have frozen hot chocolate, you know."

"Oh, I love that," Charlie said.

"You've never even had it," Simon told him. "How do you know?"

"I just know," Charlie insisted. "That's how."

"Is that right, Chuck?" Simon said. He leaned over and

messed up Charlie's hair. Charlie batted Simon's hand away and combed his hair back down with his fingers. I tried not to think about how he was sitting in my seat.

I turned to Mom. "So," I said, "can I go with Avery? She said they're leaving around eleven in the morning, and we'd probably be gone most of the day so I wouldn't bother you at all. But we won't be home too late. I mean, I'll definitely be back in Riverdale before nine thirty. Way before nine thirty." I could feel Simon looking at me from across the table, but I didn't look over at him. I knew Mom would say yes. I had already said that I didn't want to go to the city. If she didn't say yes, I would be home all day on Saturday, and then she wouldn't be able to get all her work done.

"Sure, that's fine," she said. Simon cleared his throat. I looked over and saw him raise his eyebrows at Mom from across the table, but she didn't seem to notice.

"Thanks, Mom," I said.

On Saturday morning, just after eleven o'clock, Avery called me from the car and said she and Chase were turning onto our street. "We'll be in front of your house in two minutes," she said. Simon and Charlie had already left for the city. I ran into Mom's office to say good-bye to her. Actually, it's not really an office. It's just a little alcove off the kitchen, but it's where she put her computer and desk when we moved in, so that's usually where she writes. She had printed out her manuscript so she wouldn't have to read it off the computer screen, since staring at the screen hurts her eyes, and she was bent over her manuscript, one pen behind her ear and another in her hand.

"Mom," I said. She looked up, but her eyes were kind of glazed over like she was thinking about something else even though she was looking at me. "Avery's here," I said. "I gotta go." Mom nodded and waved with the hand that wasn't holding a pen. It was so different from the last time Chase and Avery had picked me up, when Mom practically wanted to carry me out to the car. I was glad Simon was already gone, because he might have decided to walk me out and make sure Avery and Chase knew exactly what time I was supposed to be home.

This time Chase was driving a white sedan. Charlie says he likes white cars best because they're like blank pieces of paper. He says he wants a white car because then he could paint things on it. He hates that our car is dark blue.

"No sports car today?" I asked as I climbed into the backseat.

"Like my dad would ever let me take that," Chase said. "I can only take that car when he's not around. But at least we have Trixie."

"That's right," Avery said. "Good ole Trixie."

"Is Trixie what you call the car?" I asked.

"No, it's what we call the navigation system," Avery said. "You program an address in, and then a woman's voice tells you what roads to take to get there."

"We named her Trixie because her voice is so sexy," Chase added.

"I don't think her voice is so sexy," Avery said. "I think she sounds like a frog."

"Trust me," Chase said. "It's sexy. Just listen."

He punched something into a screen on the dashboard. "Right turn in approximately point two miles," a woman's voice said.

"Her voice is really deep," I said. "She almost sounds like a man."

"She does not," Chase said. "Don't listen to a word they say, Trixie."

"It sounds like Chase has a new girlfriend already," Avery said.

Chase rolled his head from side to side so his neck cracked. "Let's make this a Lizzie-free day."

"I didn't even say Lizzie's name," Avery protested.

"You just did," Chase told her. He reached over and pushed a button to turn the radio on.

"Sorry," Avery said over the music.

We got onto the highway, but this time we were headed north—away from Manhattan. Chase accelerated and I felt myself moving farther and farther away from Mom, Simon, and Charlie. I turned to look out the window and saw a silver Volkswagen Beetle go by. "Punch buggy silver," I started to say. Then I stopped myself, realizing I was probably too old for that game. When did I get too old to play punch buggy? I turned away from the window and listened to the music.

We were on the highway for over an hour, so I was startled when I heard Trixie say, "Highway exit in point five miles."

"It's about time," Avery said.

Trixie lead us off the highway and onto a twisty road with more trees and fewer cars. "It's so pretty," I said.

"Yeah, but can you imagine living up here?" Avery asked.

"There are hardly any people around. You'd be so lonely."

"I guess," I said.

"I don't know," Chase said. He was driving slower now because the road was so twisty, and I noticed little walking paths between the trees. "I think it might be nice to have this kind of privacy sometimes. Anyway, you can feel lonely even if you're in Manhattan."

"But if you're in Manhattan, you could just go outside and meet people," Avery said. "There are always things to do and people to meet."

"That's not what I meant," Chase said.

Suddenly it started to smell. "Oh, gross," Avery said. "What is that?"

"Skunk," Chase said. "Haven't you ever smelled one before?"

"No," Avery said. "But I heard the only way to make the smell go away is to take a bath in tomato juice."

"I heard that too," I said. "I've always wondered how they figured that out. Like, who was the first person to take a bath in tomato juice?"

"Maybe a long time ago some tomato farmer was sprayed by a skunk. He took a regular bath to try and wash the smell off but it didn't work, so he went to work on his tomato farm, still stinking from the skunk, and accidentally fell into a pile of tomato juice," Avery suggested.

"That seems pretty far-fetched," Chase said.

"Well, how else would you discover something like that?" Avery asked.

"I don't know," Chase said. "Maybe someone realized

that the acid from tomatoes would neutralize the smell or
something more scientific like that."

"Whatever," Avery said.

"Left turn in point two miles," Trixie said.

"Thanks, Trixie," Chase said. He slowed down to make a
left turn. "Here we are," Chase told us.

"You have arrived," Trixie said.

Chase showed us where to get baskets to collect the
apples we'd pick. He took a little map that showed what
kinds of apple trees were where and led us into the orchard.
"I think the McIntosh apples are straight back," Chase said.
"Those are the ones Mom asked us to get."

"Is she going to make a pie or something?" I asked.

"What, are you kidding?" Avery said. "I don't think my
mom remembers where the kitchen is half the time. Does
your mom cook?"

"Sometimes," I said. "Right now all she does is write
her book. She has to get it to her editor by the end of the
month."

"It's so awesome that your mom writes books," Avery
said. "Does she always dedicate them to you and Charlie?"

"No," I said. "She doesn't believe in dedicating books to
her kids."

"How come?"

"I don't know exactly," I said. "Something about privacy
and not putting our names in print. Besides, she says if she
had a regular job in an office, it's not like she would thank
her kids every time she gave a presentation."

"What's she writing about?" Chase asked.

"I'm not supposed to say. She doesn't like talking about her books until after they're done," I said.

"I wasn't about to steal her ideas," Chase said.

"It's not that," I said. "She's just superstitious. Like, if someone besides the family knows what the book is about, then she won't be able to finish it."

"Oh," Chase said.

"So, is this the same place you come to every year?" I asked. Chase nodded. I had been trying to change the subject but I realized I had made a mistake and brought up Lizzie.

"Yeah," Chase said. He shaded his eyes with his hands and looked out toward the McIntosh. I knew he was probably thinking about Lizzie. "It's this way," he said, walking faster. Avery and I followed him. Chase reached up as he walked and pulled an apple off a low-hanging branch. I watched him rub the apple against his shirt to clean it off, and then he took a bite.

"Do we have to keep track of all the apples we eat so we can pay for them later?" I asked.

"I don't think so," Avery said. "I think we only pay for the apples we take home with us. They weigh them before we go."

Chase stopped and turned to us. "I'm going to check out the Red Delicious," he said. "You guys get started on the McIntosh."

Avery picked up a pole that had been leaning against one of the trees. It had a metal hook at the top, so you could pick the apples that were out of reach. "I'm sorry my brother is so crabby," she said.

"That's all right," I said.

"My dad says you have to walk on eggshells with Chase when he gets in these moods. I guess the apple doesn't fall far from the tree, huh? Get it?" She grinned at me, and I nodded even though I had never met their father. Then I wondered about my father. Were there things I inherited from him even though I'd never met him, besides my eyes and my hair? Could you inherit a personality even if you never met someone? Maybe that was why Mom didn't understand me sometimes. Maybe if she had married my donor instead of Simon, there would be someone in the house who understood me. I sighed out loud even though I didn't mean to.

"What?" Avery asked.

"Nothing," I said. "What happened between Chase and Lizzie anyway?"

Avery shrugged. "He won't say, but it's got to be the college thing. He doesn't want to talk about her, except here we are, and I'm sure he's thinking about her."

"It's my fault," I said.

"What do you mean?" Avery asked.

"I asked Chase if this was the same place he always comes to," I said. "So now he's thinking about Lizzie again."

"No," Avery said. "He would be thinking about her even if you didn't say anything. I don't know why he wanted to come here."

"Maybe he wanted to come here to think about her," I said. "You know, maybe there were things he wanted to remember."

"I don't know," Avery said. "He's even more depressed here than he was before. It seems kind of dumb. Anyway, this looks like a good tree. Let's get some apples."

Avery and I took turns using the pole to pick apples, and we filled one of the baskets entirely with McIntosh. Then we sat down in a clearing by the trees and ate. Chase came walking back toward us, his arms filled with Red Delicious apples. "I forgot to bring one of the baskets with me," he said. Avery kicked the other basket over to him, and Chase opened his arms so the apples tumbled down into the basket.

"They're going to get all bruised," Avery said.

"Sorry," Chase said. "I'll get some more."

"And you should say sorry for being so crabby in front of Leah and then deserting us," Avery told him.

Chase looked over at me, and I blushed. "It's okay," I said quickly.

"I've got a lot on my mind," Chase said.

"All the more reason for you not to be alone," Avery told him. She pushed herself up from the ground and then wiped her palms on her jeans. "I'm going to get a couple more baskets, and then we can head over to the Golden Delicious together."

Avery ran toward the basket stand. I watched her ponytail bounce from side to side. The basket of McIntosh apples was in my lap. I wasn't sure if I was supposed to talk to Chase or leave him alone. I bent forward and pretended to count how many apples we had so far. Chase stepped toward me. I could tell because his shadow passed over my lap. "Can you hand me an apple?" he asked.

"Sure," I said.

He held out his hand and I passed him an apple. "I'm sorry if I was being a jerk," he said. "It's just with Lizzie and all of this college stuff, there's so much to figure out. And then I just get so annoyed with Avery. I'll be leaving next year, so I wanted to spend time with her. We get along better than we used to, but then she can say the most irritating things." He paused, took a bite of the apple I had handed him, chewed, and swallowed. I could see his Adam's apple move up and down. "I shouldn't be telling you these things. She's your friend. Anyway, I'm sorry."

"It's really okay," I told him. "I understand. I mean, I understand needing some space to just think."

"I don't think my sister understands that," Chase said.

"She just wants you to be happy," I said. It sounded like something my mother would say.

"I know," Chase said. "And Avery's happiest when she's surrounded by friends, and things, and noise."

"She's really popular," I said, and then I blushed again because it was such a dumb thing to say.

Chase finished his apple and threw the core toward the woods. "Yeah, and it's not like I think she's totally superficial. I mean, I've always been popular and all that. But next year I'll be somewhere else, and who knows where everyone else will be?" he said. "I don't even know for sure where I'll be."

"You don't think you'll be at Yale?" I asked.

"My parents really want me to go there. My dad went there, and his dad went there, but I might not even get in." He bent down and took another apple from the basket in my lap. When he bit into it, the juice sprayed on me a little. I tried to wipe it away without him noticing.

"So what other schools are you applying to?" I asked him. Avery came back with empty baskets on each arm, and I stood up.

"Maybe Columbia, maybe Georgetown," Chase said. "Next weekend we're going to visit Penn. The whole family is going, so I'm sure my dad will be talking about Yale the entire trip."

"I have a friend who lives near Penn," I said. "In Haverford."

"From your old school?" Avery asked.

I shook my head. Avery was still looking at me, waiting for me to explain. "It's a friend from camp," I said. I don't know what made me say that, but once I did I was happy to have thought of it. "Her name is Samantha," I continued.

"We're visiting Haverford, too," Chase said. "The college counselor says I should check it out to see what a smaller school is like. Anyway, I need another safety school."

"What's a safety school?" I asked.

"A school that's easy to get into," Avery said.

"I thought Haverford was a really good school," I said. "Not a safety." I had looked up Haverford on the Internet since talking to Samantha that first time, which was how I knew it was close to Penn. I also saw that you really need good grades to get into it.

"What's a reach school to most kids is a safety to Chase," Avery said.

"Don't start," Chase said.

"Anyway, you should totally come with us," Avery said. "You could visit your friend when we're looking at the school."

"I don't know," I said. "I don't want to intrude. It sounds like it's a family trip."

"No, you should come," Chase said. "My dad drives me crazy with all this college stuff. That's why Lizzie and I are always fighting."

"You said her name again," Avery said.

"Anyway," Chase said, ignoring Avery, "if you come, my dad might tone it down a bit."

"I'll ask my parents," I said.

Chase picked up the basket of McIntosh. He had the basket of Red Delicious on his other arm. I thought that maybe I should offer to carry one of the baskets for him since they were probably heavy, but Avery handed me one of her empty baskets. "Come on," she said, skipping ahead. I ran to catch up with her. "By the way," Avery said, "don't tell Brenna we came here today. I didn't invite her because she can be so weird around Chase sometimes. Callie's into Ian Michaelson now, but she used to be almost as bad. Just don't tell either of them about today, okay?"

"All right," I said. I turned to look back at Chase.

"Thanks," Avery said.

Now that I had a secret, I was noticing the secrets everywhere. I couldn't tell anyone what Mom was writing about, and Chase didn't want to talk about Lizzie. Now I wasn't allowed to tell Brenna and Callie about apple picking, and I didn't want to tell Avery what I was starting to think about Chase. My stomach hurt from eating so many apples and from all of the secrets.

chapterten

I t ended up being pretty easy to get Mom and Simon to let me go to Haverford. I asked them about it during dinner. Mom was so distracted by her book, she probably would have let me go to Timbuktu if it meant getting me out of the house, and Simon was fine about it since I told him Avery and Chase's parents would be with us the whole time.

I had already called Samantha to make sure she would be around that weekend. I knew she was waiting for me to call her back, so as soon as dinner was over, I ran up to my room and closed the door. It took me a while to dial because I was so excited that I misdialed a couple of times. But finally I punched in the right numbers and Samantha answered right after the first ring. "So?" she asked.

I was smiling so wide that the edges of my mouth had started to hurt. "They said yes," I said. "I'm coming."

"Oh my God! I can't believe it!"

"Me either," I said.

"I'm so excited," Samantha said. My heart was beating fast, but just then something inside me started to churn a little. I really was excited to meet Samantha, but I felt strange that I was lying to my parents about everything. I just didn't know what else to do. Even though I didn't have a choice, I felt sort of guilty. "I can't wait to meet you in person," Samantha continued. "I can't even believe that we haven't met yet. It's like I know you so well already. Isn't it funny? We're sisters and we're gonna meet for the first time."

Sisters, I repeated to myself. *We're sisters*. We were supposed to be able to see each other whenever we wanted. Mom and Simon wouldn't be mad if I were going to Haverford to visit Charlie. This was almost the same thing. "I can't wait either," I said.

A few days later we were in the white car again, headed to Pennsylvania. Trixie was programmed to the address of the admissions office at the University of Pennsylvania. This time Chase was in the backseat with Avery and me. I had volunteered to take the middle because Chase complained that his legs were too long, and Avery said it wasn't fair that she always had to sit in the middle just because she was shorter.

"Thank you, Leah," Avery's father said. No one ever told me his first name, so I wasn't sure what to call him. He seemed like someone who should be called "Sir," but I was too embarrassed to say that. Avery's mother had told me to call her Lori. I thought it would be strange to call her Lori, and then call her husband Mr. Monahan. So I called him

Mr. Monahan in my head, and out loud I didn't call him anything at all.

"No problem," I said. I had wanted to sit next to Chase anyway, and if Avery had sat in the middle, I wouldn't have been able to. But of course I didn't say that out loud. Avery would probably roll her eyes and think I had a dumb crush on Chase, just like Brenna and Callie.

But by the time Trixie told us we had arrived at the admissions office, I couldn't wait to get out of the car. It was hard to be scrunched up in the backseat for so many hours, and even though I was next to Chase, he barely talked to me. Mostly he and his father talked about Yale versus the other Ivy League colleges. Then Chase got upset, and spent the rest of the drive with his earphones on, staring out the window.

Mr. Monahan parked the car and we all got out. Chase still had his earphones stuck in his ears, and Mr. Monahan told him to take them out. He said it loudly and I was sure that Chase heard him, but Chase pretended not to hear and nodded his head to the beat of the music. Mr. Monahan reached forward and yanked on the earphones so they popped out of Chase's ears. "Chase," he hissed. "We're in front of the admissions office. You never know who's watching you. It might be the same person who ends up interviewing you. Do you really want to be the kid who had the earphones stuck in his ears?"

"Jeez, it's not as if we're at Yale," Chase said.

"Here we go again," Mr. Monahan said. He turned and walked toward the admissions office.

Chase turned to Lori. "He thinks everything I do is about Lizzie," he complained. "Sometimes I just feel like listening to music and not worrying about college."

"Come on, honey," Lori said. "You know he just wants what's best for you." She patted Chase's back and walked him toward the office. Avery and I followed behind them. It was strange to see Chase as someone's son. It made him seem so much younger. When he wasn't around his parents, he seemed more like a grown-up.

Mr. Monahan's personality changed as soon as we were inside the admissions office. He smiled and patted Chase's shoulder a lot. We were signed up for a tour of the campus, and Mr. Monahan told Avery and me that we should pay attention. "Maybe you'll want to go to school here one day," he said.

"It might be cool to go here," Avery said. "I like that it's in a city."

"Maybe that will motivate you to study harder instead of goofing off with your friends all the time," Mr. Monahan said, and he turned to me. "Avery thinks her social life is more important than her schoolwork. How are your grades, Leah?"

"They're good, I guess," I said.

"Keep it up," he told me.

Mr. Monahan went over to Chase, and I turned to Avery. I wasn't sure what to say to her, but she just shrugged, so I knew I shouldn't say anything.

The tour ended up being kind of boring. Afterward we had lunch in Philadelphia, although I wasn't really that hungry. I pushed my food around with my fork to make it look like I was eating. Finally the check came. Mr. Monahan paid and we got back into the car and headed to Haverford. I had worked out with Samantha that her mom would meet me at the admissions office and then take me to their house. The Monahans would pick me up later, after the Haverford tour.

I was used to talking to Samantha on the phone and I had been so excited about getting to meet her, but once we turned onto the Haverford campus, my heart began to race. I could feel the beats echoing in my ears. I couldn't remember ever being so nervous, and I wondered if you could have a heart attack just from being scared. I started to wish I had just stayed home, but I knew it was too late.

"Are you excited?" Avery asked me.

"About what?" I said.

"You know, about seeing your friend from camp. What's her name again?"

"Samantha," I said. My heart was still pounding, but I turned to Avery and made myself smile. I knew I had to look happy because everyone thought I was visiting a friend. I didn't want anyone to get suspicious. "I'm really excited," I said.

There was a woman standing in front of the admissions office that had to be Anna Holland, Samantha's mother. She was taller than my mom and her dark hair was twisted up on the top of her head. She was wearing a scarf even though it really wasn't cold enough for scarves. I thought maybe she was like my mom—she's always cold, even in the middle

of summer. But that didn't really make sense, because
my mom and Samantha's mom weren't even related. The
woman stared at us as we walked toward her. "Are you
Leah?" she asked.

"Yes," I said.

"Anna Holland," she said, extending a hand and smiling.
"I recognized you from your picture." It was too weird to think
about Samantha showing Anna Holland the picture I had
e-mailed her. I wondered if she had shown it to anyone else.

Anna Holland introduced herself to Avery and her family. They made arrangements to pick me up on the way
home from Haverford. I followed Ms. Holland to a parking
lot behind the admissions building, and she stopped in front
of a black car. *Charlie would be so disappointed,* I thought. And
then, thinking of Charlie, I thought about Mom and Simon.
Ms. Holland unlocked the car door and I stepped inside. I
knew I would be in major trouble if Mom or Simon found
out—I was stepping into a stranger's car. It was yet another
secret.

"I told Samantha I'd pick up a pizza," Ms. Holland said.
"But she's so excited to meet you that she said I have to drop
you off at the house first and get the pizza myself."

"I don't mind going with you," I said.

"Don't be silly," Ms. Holland said. She reached over and
patted my knee. "You know, you look a bit like Samantha."

I had stared so many times at the picture Samantha had
e-mailed me. We did both have olive skin and brown hair,
although Samantha's hair was darker than mine. I thought
Samantha was pretty, and I wanted us to look alike. Anna

Holland pulled up in front of a small white house. Samantha was waiting on the steps, and she jumped up when we pulled into the driveway. I took a deep breath before I got out of the car. I was thinking about what it would be like to walk up to the house, putting one foot in front of the other, as my heart pounded. I remembered all of my phone calls and reminded myself that Samantha wasn't a stranger. I knew her middle name now—Ellen. I knew that she wasn't named after anyone; her mother just loved the name Samantha, and she thought Ellen was a good fit as a middle name. I knew what her favorite foods were, and the names of her friends, and how she was upset about a bad grade she'd gotten in history. Still, I had never met her in person. Was I supposed to hug her hello? I wished I had figured that out before we got there.

Before I even had a chance to decide what to do, Samantha was at my side. "You're here!" she squealed. "Oh, God, I can't believe it!"

"I know," I said. "I can't believe it either."

We stood there staring at each other for a few seconds, and then Ms. Holland called to us from the other side of the car. "Sorry to interrupt," she said, "but I'm headed out for the pizza now. Is there anything else I should pick up?"

Samantha looked at me. "I'm fine, thanks," I said. Actually, I wasn't even hungry for pizza. I was still too nervous and excited to be hungry for anything.

"We're good, Mom," Samantha said. She grabbed my hand and pulled me toward the house. "I can't wait to show you everything!" she told me.

We walked up the front steps. There was a BEWARE OF DOG

sign in the front window, and I hesitated for a second. When I was younger, we had a neighbor with a German shepherd. The dog had gotten loose once when I was playing in the front yard. It ran over to me and knocked me down. Even though I wasn't hurt, I haven't really liked dogs since then. Samantha had never mentioned a dog in any of our phone conversations. "Do you have a dog?" I asked.

"No," Samantha said. "We used to, but she died a few years ago, and we didn't even have the sign back then. But there was a robbery in our neighborhood, and my mom thought that maybe having a 'Beware of Dog' sign would scare the robbers away."

"Have you ever been robbed?" I asked.

"Nope," Samantha said. "Maybe the sign is working."

We walked inside and Samantha gave me a quick tour of the downstairs. Then we headed upstairs so I could see her room. I think you can tell a lot about a person by her room. My room is filled with bookshelves because I read so much. Also, Mom framed some of my best drawings, and they're hanging on the wall across from my bed. I followed Samantha to a room at the end of the hall. The door was partway open and she pushed it all the way open.

The first thing I noticed was how messy her room was. "Sorry," Samantha said, kicking aside a pile of clothes on the floor. "My mom said I should clean before you got here, and I really meant to. But then I thought that since we're getting to know each other, you may as well find out now that I'm a slob."

"It's not so bad," I said.

"Yeah, right," Samantha said. "You're a terrible liar!" We both laughed. Samantha said she wanted to show me her pictures. She cleared a place on the bed for me to sit down and pulled a couple photo albums off of a shelf. "These are from the last couple years of school," she told me. She pointed out her best friend, a girl named Arielle with curly brown hair.

"Does she know about you?" I asked. "I mean, does she know you have a donor?"

"Of course," Samantha said. "She knows everything about me."

I felt my heart start to beat faster again. There wasn't anyone in the world who knew everything about me. Mom and Simon didn't even know where I was, and I was trying so hard to be normal that I hadn't told Avery anything about having a donor. I had even lied to her about who Samantha was. Samantha was the closest to knowing everything about me, and I had just met her. It made me feel lonely.

Samantha turned the page of the photo album. "These are my glamour shots," she said, pointing toward more pictures of her. She was standing against a low brick wall with her hand on her hip. Her hair was blowing in the wind. "Sometimes Arielle and I pretend to be models and take pictures of each other."

"You look really pretty," I said.

"Thanks," she said. "I think I sort of look like you in this one." I looked closely at the picture she was pointing to. The sun was shining on the top of her head, so her hair looked a little lighter.

"It does sort of look like me," I said.

I stared at Samantha's features—two green eyes, a narrow nose with a slight bump in the middle, and a mouth that curved up a little higher on one side than on the other. I remembered how Mom had looked through books of potential donors at Lyon's Reproductive Services, trying to decide what features she would like best for her future child. Anna Holland had gone to Lyon's too. She had picked out the same features. Now Samantha and I were together, sitting on her bed.

Samantha flipped the page in her photo album. "And here I am with the boys," she said. I sat forward and followed Samantha's finger to a picture in the center of the page. "That's Andrew and Henry. They're brothers, you know. Twins, actually. But they're fraternal twins so they look a little different. And Tate's the little one. We all met up a few months ago. Andrew was in this big football tournament, and his team was playing near Tate's house. They invited my mom and me to come watch too. I'm not really into football, but it was fun to see everyone. They even won the game." In the picture Samantha had her arm around Tate's shoulder. She looked just as casual and comfortable as I look in the pictures of Charlie and me.

"What're they like?" I asked.

"Oh, they're fun," Samantha said. "Andrew and Henry are really into sports. Henry's a little more serious than Andrew, and Tate's a total goofball. He's always e-mailing me jokes. Like, every couple of days I get another joke from him. I'm sure he'd e-mail them to you if you write him, or I could forward them to you, if you want."

"Thanks," I said. We heard a car drive up, and then Samantha's mother called from downstairs to let us know she was home with the pizza. Samantha closed the photo album and tossed it aside. I wanted to pick it up and put it back on the shelf, but I didn't know her well enough to clean her room for her. She would probably think that was rude.

"Come on," Samantha said. "I can practically taste the pizza already."

We went down to the kitchen. The pizza did smell good. I wasn't as nervous anymore so I was actually a little bit hungry. "I forgot to ask you what you liked on your pizza," Ms. Holland said. "So I got half plain and half pepperoni—that's Samantha's favorite."

"I'll take a slice of pepperoni, please," I said. Samantha grinned at me. Ms. Holland brought me a slice and sat down next to me. Samantha was on the other side. I could feel them looking at me, but I didn't mind it. Actually, it sort of made me feel better because I felt like I was staring at them too.

"So, Leah," Ms. Holland said. "Tell us about your family." Samantha already knew about them, but I told Ms. Holland about Mom marrying Simon, and all about Charlie. "I'd love to meet them," Ms. Holland said.

"They don't exactly know that Leah is here," Samantha told her. Ms. Holland raised her eyebrows.

"I just don't know what they would think," I told her.

"What do you mean?" Ms. Holland asked.

"Well, they might be mad at me. They think we have this perfect family. Simon adopted me, and I don't think they even remember that I have a donor. At least, they usually act like they don't remember it."

"I think your parents would want to know where you are," Ms. Holland said. I hoped Ms. Holland wouldn't want to call them herself to let them know where I was. If Mom and Simon knew I was with Samantha, they would jump into the car to come and get me. They would ground me for the rest of the year.

"They know I'm in Haverford," I said. "They said it was okay for me to go with Avery. I just didn't tell them I was coming to your house." I watched Ms. Holland to see if she was going to stand up and reach for the phone, but she just kept eating her pizza.

My cell phone rang after a little while. I was still thinking about Mom and Simon, and I practically jumped out of my seat. For a second I worried that it was one of them, calling to check up on me. But then I recognized the beat of one of the songs Avery had programmed into it. It had to be Avery calling. "We're leaving the campus now," she told me. "We should be there soon." I hung up and told Samantha and her mother that I was getting picked up in a few minutes.

"I wish you could stay for the rest of the weekend," Samantha said.

"Me too," I told her.

"Maybe next time," Ms. Holland said. "You have an open invitation to visit us, so tell your parents and come back anytime."

"Thanks," I said, even though I knew I couldn't tell Mom or Simon.

A few minutes later the Monahans pulled up outside the house. Samantha walked me to the front door. She had slipped her arm through mine. I noticed that the hallway was painted yellow, and it looked extra bright when the sun streamed in through the front window with the BEWARE OF DOG sign. I thought about how I would always remember it, even if I never came back. Maybe we really could arrange to go to camp together. I would ask Samantha what camp she went to and then tell Mom I had heard about a new camp that I wanted to try. I could spend the whole summer with Samantha, and afterward I could visit her in Haverford and even invite her to stay with us in Riverdale. Mom and Simon would never have to know the truth.

We hugged good-bye. I tried not to make a big deal out of it because Avery and her family were watching. Samantha knew I had told them that we went to camp together, so when I got into the car, Samantha said, "See you this summer."

"See you," I said. I felt my eyes getting hot and I swallowed hard. I wiped my eyes quickly, hoping no one would notice.

"Are you okay?" Avery asked. I nodded. "I always get upset when I leave my camp friends," she said. "I cry and cry, like they're the only friends I have in the world. It's like when I'm away at camp, I forget about everyone home in Riverdale. And then I go back to school and I stop missing my camp friends so much."

"I'm okay," I said.

"I know," Avery told me. "After all, you have me."

chaptereleven

S amantha started calling me "sister." We were on the phone one night, and in the background I heard Ms. Holland calling her. Samantha held the phone away from her mouth, but she shouted so I could still hear her. "Hold on, Ma," she said. "I'm on the phone with my sister."

I had thought a lot about how we were sisters, but I never said it out loud like that, like a title—like the way I talked about Charlie and said, "I have to pick my brother up from school." Samantha came back on and started talking about something she and Arielle had done the night before, but I let the words roll around in my head—*I'm on the phone with my sister, my sister, my sister.*

The next time Samantha called, I answered the phone and she said, "Hey, Sis!"

"Hey, Sis," I said back. I tried to sound breezy like Samantha had, like the words just rolled off my tongue. But it still sounded strange. Charlie wandered into my room and wanted to know who I was talking to. "Just a friend," I told him.

"Is it Avery?" He climbed up onto the bed and bent toward the phone. "Hello, Avery!" he shouted. "I saw a giant!"

"Go away," I told him. I don't usually say things like that to Charlie. But I was talking to Samantha and I didn't want him hanging around. If he overheard anything about the Lyon's Sibling Registry or my visiting Samantha, he might go ask Mom or Simon about it.

Charlie looked up at me and pouted. "I just wanted to say hello," he said.

"It's not Avery," I said. "It's my friend Samantha and you don't know her."

"But I need your help with something," Charlie said. "When will you be off the phone?"

"I don't know, Charlie," I said. "Go ask Mom for help." Charlie climbed off the bed, shoulders rounded. I told him to shut the door on his way out. "Sorry about that," I said to Samantha.

"I wish you would tell him about me," she said.

"What about you?" I asked, even though I knew what she meant: She wanted me to tell Charlie that she was my sister.

"You know," Samantha said. "That we're related. That I'm your sister."

"I can't," I said. "Charlie wouldn't understand everything."

"You don't have to explain *everything* to him," Samantha said. "But you're always saying how smart he is, and he already knows that Simon isn't your real dad. Couldn't you tell him about me a little bit at least?"

"No, I really can't," I said.

"You act like the world will blow up or something if you tell anyone in your family about me."

"I don't think the world will blow up," I said.

"Well, not literally blow up," Samantha said. "But you're always talking about how mad your parents would be, and you really don't know that for sure. When I told my mom about the Lyon's Sibling Registry, she wasn't mad at all. She thought it was fine for me to find out about having siblings, and she liked meeting the boys and you."

I could tell Samantha was hurt because I was keeping her a secret. "I'm sorry," I said. "I can't tell my parents, and if I tell Charlie, he'll just tell my parents, and if they find out, they'll really flip. They're not like your mom. I really think they'd go crazy if they found out I used their credit card and went to a stranger's house in Haverford."

"I'm not a stranger," Samantha insisted.

"Not to me," I said. "But you are to them. If I tell them, they might say I'm not allowed to talk to you anymore."

Samantha was quiet for a moment, which doesn't usually happen. Finally she said, "God, that would suck."

"I know," I said.

I had actually started to feel like I needed to talk to Samantha. We spoke a couple of times a week, usually sometime after dinner when I was up in my room doing my homework. She would call or I would call her, and we would talk about the things that had happened in school, or something good on television that one of us had seen, or something annoying that one of our parents had done. I didn't have to pretend about anything when I was talking to her. Maybe that was what it was really like to have a sister—well, at least a half sister who lived in a different state. Having a brother was entirely different. Charlie was too young for me to really talk to him like that. Most of my conversations with Charlie were about Charlie, or things that Charlie liked. He wasn't old enough for me to explain the things I was thinking about. Besides, he wasn't a girl, so even if he were older, I didn't think I'd be able to talk to him the same way.

But maybe it wasn't just that Samantha and I were related. Callie and her sister, Megan, barely spoke to each other. Callie never even introduced me to her, but I knew who she was because Brenna told me. Brenna and I had been walking down the hall, and she'd waved at someone, who she told me was Callie's sister, Megan. Then she told me, once they were all having dinner at Callie's apartment, and when Megan wanted the salt she said, "Brenna, can you please ask Callie to pass the salt?" And so Brenna asked her, and then Callie said, "Of course, Brenna, and can you please ask Megan to pass the bread?" Brenna said they both spoke in really thick, syrupy voices so you knew they were just faking being nice. She said it was obvious they hated each other. But since I had never been to Callie's apartment, I hadn't ever actually seen them together. It was crazy, because Callie and Megan really did look so much alike. They looked like sisters who should have a lot in common and get along.

Samantha stopped being upset about my not telling Mom and Simon about her. She was telling me about something she and Arielle had seen at the mall. Charlie came back into my room. I hate when he comes in without knocking. Sometimes he does it in the morning when I'm getting dressed. I've started to feel weird about changing in front of Charlie. He notices things more, now that he's five. The other day he told me my boobs looked bigger. My face turned red. I crossed my arms in front of my chest and called to Mom so she would make him leave. But I think maybe I wouldn't mind changing in front of a sister.

At least this time I was fully dressed. Charlie shuffled over to the bed wearing his blue Thomas the Tank Engine pajamas. "You're still on the phone," he said. I nodded. Samantha was talking about a sweater that Anna Holland said was too expensive. "Mom says it's bedtime soon, and I still need your help," Charlie said.

I held up two fingers to signal to Charlie to give me a couple seconds. That's what Mom does when she's on the phone. Sometimes she also mouths the words "two seconds." Charlie leaned against me. "Two seconds," he said softly. Then he raised his voice: "One, two! Two seconds is over!" I covered his mouth with my hand. I could feel the air coming out of his nose as he breathed in and out. If it were anyone else, I would have thought it was gross, but I didn't mind Charlie's breath. I waited for Samantha to finish talking. She said the sweater was so soft it was probably cashmere.

"Maybe she'll surprise you with it," I said.

Samantha snorted. "My mom may be cool about some things, but she's definitely not cool about clothing. She thinks the only purpose of clothing is to cover you up and keep you warm."

"That's too bad," I said. Charlie nudged me. "Anyway, I have to go. Charlie just came in here again."

"Will you tell him I say hello?" Samantha asked.

"Okay," I told her. We said good-bye. I hung up and looked down at Charlie. "Samantha said hello to you, by the way."

"Who's Samantha?" Charlie asked.

"My friend that I was just talking to," I told him.

"Oh, yeah," Charlie said.

He leaned into me a little more and lifted a hand up to play with my hair. "Don't you think it would be funny if I had really long hair?" he said. "There's a boy in my class with long hair. It's almost as long as yours and he looks like a girl. But he's not a girl, even though he has a girl's name."

"What's his name?"

"Casey," Charlie said.

"Casey can be a boy or a girl," I said.

"I know two girls named Casey and only one boy named Casey, so I think it's really a girl's name," Charlie said.

"What did you need my help with?" I asked him.

I shifted my weight, and Charlie sat up. "Daddy bought me more poster board."

"What are you talking about?"

"For my family tree," Charlie said impatiently, and he looked at me the way Mom does sometimes when she thinks I'm being exasperating.

"I thought Family Month was over," I said. "You already made a poster—with Mom, remember?"

"Yeah, but I have to make another one. Aaron in my class made one that's better than mine. Mrs. Trager's always saying 'Look what Aaron drew,' or 'Aaron did a very nice job on this project,' and it's not fair because you didn't even help me, so mine wasn't good enough."

"So Aaron's the teacher's pet," I said.

"What do you mean?"

"Nothing," I said. I thought about how Charlie is probably much smarter than any other kid in his class. I didn't say that out loud, though, because Mom and Simon don't want Charlie to feel self-conscious about his genius IQ.

"Aaron's poster has lots of different colors," Charlie said. "The leaves are all different colors and not just green. It has red and orange and blue. Mrs. Trager said it looks like a tree in autumn."

"I've never seen a tree with blue leaves," I said. "Not even in autumn."

"Come on, dude," Charlie said. He stood up and pulled my hand. Sometimes when Mom is sitting down and Charlie wants her to do something, she holds out her hand and says, "Help me. I'm getting too old to stand up by myself." So Charlie will pull her arm, and he thinks he's really helping. He forgets all the times she stands up by herself with no help at all.

"Dude? Do I look like a dude to you?"

"Aaron calls everyone dude," Charlie explained.

"Well, girls aren't dudes," I told him.

"All right," Charlie said. "Then you can be a dudette." He pulled my arm harder and led me down the hall. He was walking on his tiptoes, which he does sometimes because he wants to be taller. His preschool teacher made Mom take him to a foot doctor to make sure nothing was wrong with the arches of his feet. Charlie was upset because the doctor told him that he needed to walk with his feet flat on the ground. We're supposed to remind him when we see him walking on his tiptoes.

"Charlie," I said, "watch your feet."

"I was being a giant," he said. "Daddy and I saw a real live giant at the poster store. Like Jack and the Beanstalk."

"Really?"

"Yeah. Daddy said he was probably about eight feet tall. He was much, much taller than Daddy is." Simon is pretty tall himself, so it was hard to imagine someone who was much taller. "You know," Charlie continued, "I sort of felt bad for the giant. Everyone was staring at him because he was so big. Daddy made me walk down another aisle because it's not nice to stare. But I looked back around when Daddy wasn't looking, and I saw that the giant had to duck when he was leaving the store because he was even taller than the door. I wonder if he has to go to special stores for giants to get clothes and shoes. He had really big feet, too. And really, really big hands. Do you think he needs a special car? I bet he wouldn't even fit in our car."

"I don't know," I said. "I've never seen anything special-made for giants." If Mom or Simon were there, they would have made a big deal about how much harder it was for the giant to be so tall than it was for Charlie to be a little bit on the small side, and they'd make sure to tell him that he shouldn't feel so bad about being short. But I don't think everything needs to be turned into a lesson, and besides, I think Charlie already knew all of that. Of course he didn't have it as bad as the giant, but he still wanted to be a regular-size kid.

"Can we start drawing the tree now?" Charlie asked.

"Yes," I said.

The poster board was too big to fit on Charlie's desk, so we sat on the floor. "I have lots of different colors," Charlie said, handing me his bucket of markers and crayons.

"I just need a pencil right now," I said. "First I have to sketch it, and then we can color it in."

Charlie got up to get a pencil from his desk. "But when we color it, we need lots of colors because Aaron had a lot of colors."

"I know," I said. "Don't worry."

I started drawing Charlie in the center of the page, his arms outstretched above his head. Charlie sat on his knees and leaned forward so his shadow crossed my sketch. "That doesn't look right," he said. "It's supposed to be a tree."

"I know," I said. "I'm going to make it so you are in the middle, like the trunk of a tree, and then your arms will be two branches, one for Mom and one for Dad."

"But what about everybody else?"

"We'll keep drawing branches growing from the branches," I explained. "So Dad's branch will split into two more branches for Grandma Diane and Grandpa Willie, and Mom's branch will split into two more branches for Grandma Leah and Grandpa Izzy. And the branches will keep splitting until we've drawn branches for everyone. So it will be a family tree with you right there in the middle."

"Awesome," Charlie said.

"Move over a little," I told him. "It's hard to see where I'm drawing when you lean over the poster like that."

"Sorry," Charlie said. "I just wanna see."

I bent forward and got to work. I drew Charlie so his legs looked like roots and his arms were branches. His left arm was for Mom and his right arm was for Simon. I drew branches for everyone else—Charlie's grandparents, aunts, uncles, and cousins. Then I made another branch off to the side, extending down from Mom's branch, for me. I wrote my name in a box next to the branch and thought it looked sort of lonely. It was strange how I had just been on the phone with Samantha and she had called me her sister, and then I was drawing my brother's family tree and she wasn't on it. I sat back and looked at Charlie. "What do you think?" I asked him.

"It's way better than Aaron's," Charlie said. "Well, it will be when it's all colored in."

"Good," I said.

"You're so good at drawing," Charlie said.

"Thank you," I said.

"I wish I could draw like that," he said.

"Hey, Charlie," I said. "Do you think you'd want to meet my friend Samantha one day?"

"Can she come get ice cream with us?"

"Maybe," I said. "Maybe pizza, too. I think you'd really like her."

"Okay," Charlie said.

There was a knock at the door. We turned, and Mom was standing against the door frame. "It's bedtime, Charlie," she said.

"We're making my family tree," Charlie said.

"I see that," Mom said. "But you still have to go to bed now."

"But we're not finished yet," he said. "It's not colored in."

"It's okay," I said. "We can finish it tomorrow." I thought about Samantha and my other donor siblings. Did they belong on Charlie's family tree if they were related to me and not to him? The tree looked a little empty without them.

"Come on, Char-Char," Mom said. "Pick out a couple books and I'll read to you." Charlie went to his bookshelf while I rolled the poster up. Mom picked up the bucket of markers and crayons and put it back on Charlie's desk.

I walked out of the room and heard Charlie asking Mom, "Did Daddy tell you about the giant we saw?"

chaptertwelve

T he next day, I came home from school and Mom was sitting on the front stoop. When I started up the driveway in front of our house, she stood up, and I began to walk faster. Why wasn't Mom at Charlie's school picking him up? Did something horrible happen to him? Had she asked me to pick him up and I'd forgotten? Was he all alone and crying? It's funny how many things can pop into your head all at once when you're scared. Then I remembered he had a playdate with his friend Brandon. Mom and Simon had been making fun of the word "playdate" the night before. They said when they were young, they never had "dates" to "play." Their parents just let them out of the house to play with other kids in the neighborhood, and then around dinnertime all the kids would go home. They were talking the way grown-ups talk sometimes about the way things used to be—as though it were better back then, even though I know they like things the way they are and they would never actually let Charlie just leave the house to play with other kids. They would want to know exactly where he was, and how he was getting there, and how he was getting home, and who the parents were.

I stepped up to the stoop where Mom was standing. She was clutching a piece of paper. I thought maybe it was something about her book because she was holding it against her chest like it was something important. "I was waiting for you," she said.

"What's going on?" I asked.

"You tell me," Mom said.

"What do you mean?" I asked.

"The credit card bill came this morning," Mom said. She extended her arm and waved the paper toward me. I recognized the credit card logo at the top—the same logo is on the credit card that Mom and Simon had given to me. It was the credit card I had used to sign up for the Lyon's Sibling Registry. When I tried to breathe in, the breath seemed to catch in my throat. "Is there anything you want to tell me about?" Mom asked.

Up until that moment, I had stopped worrying so much about the credit card bill. Mom and Simon hadn't mentioned anything about it, and it had been almost three months since I had signed up for the Lyon's Sibling Registry. I figured the bill had come and gone and they just hadn't noticed it. But there was Mom standing in front of me, waving the credit card bill. Isn't that always how it happens? You think you're off the hook and you let your guard down, and things blow up in your face. I shook my head. There wasn't anything I wanted to tell her. All I wanted was to go straight up to my room and hide under the covers. I wasn't sure I would ever want to tell her about anything ever again. I braced myself for her to start yelling.

"Come on, Leah," Mom said, putting her hand on my elbow. "Let's go inside and talk about this."

I followed Mom to the dining room table, and I sat in the chair that used to be mine, before Charlie traded without asking me first. Now he wasn't there and I wished he were, because then maybe Mom would be too distracted by him to stare at me the way she was. Mom said that the credit card bill had arrived that morning. "I saw the Lyon's Sibling Registry charge," she said. "I thought it must be a mistake, so I called the credit card company and they said it was a monthly charge. They said someone had signed up on your card several months ago."

My elbows were propped up on the table. I rested my chin in my palm and I looked down. There was a line of purple marker on the table that had been there for years. Mom had always told me to put newspaper down on the table if I was going to color, so I didn't get marker on the wood, but I had forgotten once. I'd been Charlie's age, and Mom had gone nuts because I'd ruined the table that used to belong to her parents. I kept telling her it was an accident, but she didn't care. She sent me to my room, and when I snuck out later on, I saw her bent over the table scrubbing hard. It looked like she was crying.

"I've just been so busy with my book," Mom continued. "I haven't been paying all that much attention to the bills when they come in. I didn't look at the individual charges. I wrote out checks and sent them in. But the book's handed in now, so when I opened the bill today, I looked at it more carefully. And after I spoke to the credit card company, I went through the old bills. They were right, you know. I guess you know that. You signed up two months ago. We've been getting charged all along."

I lowered my face into my hands. My palms were sweaty again, and my cheeks felt hot against them. I hadn't realized the Sibling Registry was a monthly charge. Maybe it was in all that legal stuff I hadn't read. I wished I'd read more carefully. I would've canceled my registration as soon as I got Samantha's phone number. Then the charge wouldn't have been on the bill when it came today, and Mom would never have found out.

"Look up, Leah," Mom said. She didn't sound angry. I kept waiting for her to start yelling, but her voice had been soft and even when she told me about the credit card bill, and calling the company, and going through all the old bills. I raised my head. "I understand that you're curious about all this," Mom said.

I hated that she used the word "curious." It seemed like such a dumb word—a little-kid word. Like the Curious George books that Charlie liked to read at bedtime. *Curious George Visits the Zoo. Curious George Goes to the Beach. Curious George Takes a Trip.* "Curious" was not the right word for a teenager who had just discovered new siblings. Even though Mom wasn't yelling at me, I knew she didn't understand anything I was feeling. "I don't want to talk about it," I said.

"I know," Mom said. "But we need to talk about it. We can't just ignore it."

"I'm not ignoring it," I said. "I just don't want to talk about it with you."

"Will you talk about it with Simon, then?" Mom asked.

"No way," I said.

Mom breathed in deeply and pressed her fingertips into

her temples like she had a headache. She closed her eyes for a moment and pressed harder so the tips of her fingers turned white. Then she put her hands back down and opened her eyes. "You have to talk to one of us," she said.

"I don't know what you want me to say," I said. "I'm sorry I used the credit card without permission."

But I wasn't really sorry about using the credit card. I was glad about it—otherwise I wouldn't have found Samantha.

"This isn't about the credit card," Mom said.

"Then, what is it about?" I asked.

"It's about the website, Leah," Mom said. "And why you went on it, and what you're curious about." There was that word again. I wished Mom would just stop talking, but she continued. "Did you find anyone related to Donor 730? I saw the links for the donors, but I couldn't click on them without paying for it. I guess you know that."

"You went on the website?" I asked. It seemed like such an invasion of privacy, even though anyone with a computer could get on the website, and anyone with a credit card could sign up and access the information.

"Of course I did," she said. I felt my cheeks flush—*of course*. She made it sound so simple. "Did you find anyone?" she asked again.

"Yes," I said.

"Who?" Mom asked.

"Four kids," I said.

"Boys or girls?"

"Both."

"Leah," Mom said, "this feels like pulling teeth. You're

only giving me one-word answers. Can you give me a little more here?"

I had given her a two-word answer when I'd said "four kids," but I didn't correct her. "Three boys and a girl," I told her, which was five words. Mom nodded, waiting for me to say more. "The girl's name is Samantha. She's exactly my age." I repeated it in my head and counted nine more words. That was enough.

"Hmm," Mom said, rubbing at her temples again, but this time not as hard. I thought about offering to get her some aspirin. I didn't really want to be nice to her, but I didn't really want to keep sitting with her at the table.

"Do you have a headache?" I said. "I'll go get you some aspirin."

I started to stand, but Mom moved her hand from her temple and put it on my arm. "No, no," she said. "I'm just thinking." The heat from her hand on my arm made me feel trapped. "Maybe one day you can meet Samantha," Mom said.

"One day?" I asked.

"Yes," Mom said. "When you're older, if you're still curious. Maybe then you can."

"Why do I have to wait?"

"We don't even know where she lives," Mom said.

"*I* know where she lives," I told her.

"Well, I still think it's a little too much for right now," she said. "You're only thirteen and have so much going on already—a new school, new friends. You have final exams coming up. I don't want this to interfere with what's really important."

"This is important," I said.

"Leah," Mom said. She rubbed her hand up and down my arm. It was too hot and I pulled away.

"I already met her," I said.

"When?"

"When I went with Avery and her family to see colleges. Samantha's mom works at Haverford."

"Were Avery's parents with you?"

I thought about telling her that they were with me the whole time, but what if she met Lori and asked her about it, and Lori told her how it had really happened? "No," I said. "They took a tour of the school and I had lunch with Samantha and her mom."

"You had lunch by yourself with strangers?"

"They're not strangers," I said. "They're family."

"No," Mom said. "They aren't family."

"She's my sister." I said the word with confidence, just like Samantha always does. I wished Samantha were there to hear me.

"She's not your sister," Mom said. "All you share is a donor."

"Then Charlie's not my brother," I told her. "All we share is a mother."

"You don't really believe that," Mom said. "That all you share is me? You've been so much to each other. You've been like another mother to him, and he needs you so much. You've grown up together. That's what being a brother or a sister is."

We sat there, silent. It seemed like a really long time. I heard cars passing outside the house, and the *tick, tick, tick* sound of the clock in the kitchen. It's bright red and shaped like a cat. The tail wags back and forth with the *tick, tick, tick* sound. Charlie had picked it out as a Mother's Day gift. I knew Mom didn't really like it, but she had to keep it since it was from Charlie. She had taken the battery out while she was writing because her office is so close to the kitchen and the ticking sound distracted her. I guess she had put the battery back in. Finally Mom reached out toward me again. "Come on," she said. "The proofs for my book came and I want to show you something."

She stood up and looked down at me, like everything I said didn't count. She was moving on, changing the subject, just like we do when we want to distract Charlie. Why couldn't she realize that I wasn't a little kid? I could make decisions for myself. I could stay out late. I could decide who was and wasn't my sister.

"Your book," I said, standing up. I felt my eyes beginning to fill, and I bit the inside of my cheek so I wouldn't cry. "It's a total lie."

"What are you talking about?"

"*How to Talk So Your Parents Will Listen?* What a joke! You never listen to me!"

"Why can't we ever just have a conversation? Why are you turning everything into a battle?"

I didn't answer. I just picked up my backpack and ran to the door.

chapterthirteen

I rang the doorbell at Avery's house, and a few seconds later I heard footsteps, and then Lori was there, ushering me in, taking my backpack, calling for Avery.

We sat down in the den. Lori had given me a box of tissues, and I had a tissue balled in my fist. I felt it getting gross and shredded because my hands were so sweaty. Avery reached for my other hand but I pretended not to see her. I didn't want her to feel how wet my hand was. Lori leaned forward and put her hand on my knee. "Do you want to talk about it, honey?"

I shook my head.

"I used to fight with my mother a lot when I was your age," Lori said. "She had a lot on her mind. I didn't have a father around and my mother was so worried all of the time. It was hard for us kids to understand all of that. I was the oldest, so she expected a lot from me. But even when you're the oldest kid, you're still a kid. Sometimes parents lose sight of that."

"Leah's the oldest too," Avery said. "Her brother is eight years younger."

"Just like my sister Sarah," Lori said. "She's seven and a half years younger than I am. When I was a teenager,

Sarah was always following me around. I'd tell her to leave me alone, but my mother would tell me I had to take care of Sarah. I still remember all of the fights with my mother, with her telling me I wasn't allowed to leave my sister out. Sometimes I hear myself doing that to Chase."

"Mo-om!" Avery said.

"I know, honey," Lori said. She lifted her hand from my knee to pat Avery. "And I don't think Chase minds having you around. I'm just saying that sometimes it's nice for an older sibling to have some time alone. With Sarah and me, well, I just wanted a moment not to think about her. But my mom never let me forget my sister."

"But that's just it," I said. "My mom wants me to forget all about my sister!"

The words just came out. It happens sometimes, when I'm all worked up about something. I squeezed my eyes shut so I wouldn't have to look at Avery or Lori.

"You mean your brother," Avery said. "You mean Charlie, right?"

I knew I could lie, right then. It would be so easy. I could say I meant my brother. I meant Charlie. And they would think it was because I was so upset and messed up that I'd just gotten confused and said the wrong word. I opened my eyes and saw Avery and Lori both expecting me to say that I meant Charlie. I started to nod, but it all seemed so stupid, pretending Samantha didn't exist, pretending I was just like other kids. That's what Mom and I were fighting about. I didn't want to pretend anymore. "No," I said. "I meant my sister."

When Avery is having a hard time figuring something

out, she gets a line like a little parenthesis right next to her eyebrow. I noticed it once when our math teacher, Mrs. Simmons, called on her and she didn't know the answer. The little parenthesis popped up next to her eyebrow just then. She was trying to figure it out. "Did she die?" Avery asked.

"What?"

"Did you have a sister who died?" she asked. "Like a twin or something? And your mom just wants to forget about it because it's so painful to remember? Is that why you're fighting?"

"Avery," Lori said, saying her name like a warning. But she was leaning forward, toward me, and I could tell she wanted to know the answer.

"No, she isn't dead," I said.

"I don't understand," Avery said. "I didn't even know you had a sister. All you ever talk about is Charlie."

"I know," I said. "It's really complicated. She doesn't live with us."

"Where does she live?" Avery asked. I didn't answer right away. I just watched Avery watching me. I knew she was imagining all sorts of crazy scenarios. It wasn't a dead sister, but maybe it was a sister who was sick and living in a hospital, a sister who was crazy and locked up in an institution, a sister who was put up for adoption, a sister who lived in Europe with my long-lost father.

Everything seemed so quiet all of a sudden. I just kept looking at Avery looking at me. The parenthesis was still next to her eyebrow, and there was a really faint scar right by her left ear. I hadn't ever noticed it before, but I saw it when she moved her hands to her face and pulled her hair back. She twisted her hair at the back of her head and knotted it. She has such long hair that she can loop it around, make a knot, and pull a ponytail through. I've tried to do it with my hair, but the knot always falls apart.

Lori coughed and the sound startled me, but then it didn't seem so quiet anymore. The phone was ringing. I heard footsteps from the floor above us, probably Chase going to answer the phone. Avery shifted and the leather on the couch made a crunchy noise. "She lives in Haverford," I said finally.

"Haverford? Really? Why didn't you tell me? We were just there! We could have seen her!"

"But I did see her," I said.

Avery scrunched her face like she was thinking, and I could tell she was confused, but Lori nodded. "Your friend from camp," Lori said.

"Yes," I said.

"She's your sister?" Avery asked.

"My half sister, actually," I said.

"Of course," Avery said. "You have different mothers, and your mom must hate your father for moving so far away, so she doesn't want you to see your sister."

I shook my head. "You're going to think I'm so messed up," I said.

"I won't," Avery said. "You can trust me."

"It's all right, honey," Lori said.

I took a deep breath in and let it out slowly, and then I started to tell them—about Mom going to Lyon's Reproductive Services and choosing my donor. I told them how I had found the Lyon's Sibling Registry on the Internet and read about Samantha and the boys, our half brothers. I told them how Samantha and I talked on the phone and how she called me her sister. Avery was looking at me closely but I wasn't sure what she was thinking. She didn't look upset or disgusted. I knew she probably wouldn't be rude to me in front of Lori, but we had to go to school the next day and Lori wouldn't be there. Maybe Avery would stop wanting to hang out with me so much. Maybe she wouldn't invite me to sit with her, Brenna, and Callie at lunch anymore. It was too late for me to try to be normal anymore.

"Oh, honey," Lori said when I'd finished. "That's very tough. I'm so sorry."

"I'm sorry too," Avery said.

"Well," Lori said, "how about if I go make some hot chocolate or something? That always used to make me feel better."

"That'd be good, Mom," Avery said.

Lori stood up and pulled at her shirt to straighten the creases. I watched her walk out of the room. Avery was right there next to me, but I didn't know what to say. "You like hot chocolate, right?" Avery asked.

"I thought your mom didn't know how to make anything," I said.

"She can make hot chocolate in the microwave," Avery said. "And she can make that macaroni with the powdered cheese that comes in a box. That's about all she can make."

"Oh," I said.

"But we make some pretty mean chocolate chip cookies, don't you think?"

"Yes, I guess we do," I said.

"Just for the record, I don't think you're messed up," Avery said. She had pulled out the knot in her hair so that her hair fell over her shoulders. She looked sweet and sincere, but I wasn't sure that I believed her. Then, like she could read my mind, she said, "Believe me, Leah. I swear."

I almost nodded, but Avery started to laugh. *I knew it*, I thought. *I knew she didn't mean it.*

"I'm not laughing at you," she said, reading my mind again.

"It's okay," I said.

"But I'm really not laughing at you," she insisted.

"Then, what are you laughing at?"

"Well, it's just that you wouldn't believe what I was making up in my head when you said you had a secret sister. I thought maybe she was in some insane asylum and so it was a big family secret. Then I thought maybe she had some horrible disease, like maybe she was a leper or something. We learned about the lepers last year. You know, they used to ship them off to these far-off islands to die, and the families would pretend they never knew them in the first place." I smiled because I realized that I could read Avery's mind too. I knew she had been making up crazy things in her head. "So I guess you think that *I'm* the one who's messed up," Avery said.

"No, I think we're even," I said.

"Good," Avery said. "Even though I wouldn't really care if you thought I was messed up. So, what's she like anyway?"

"Do you mean Samantha?"

"Yeah, of course I mean Samantha."

"Well," I said, "she's nice. She likes shopping. I think she's probably popular. She talks a lot."

"*I* talk a lot," Avery said.

"She talks even more than you do," I said.

I expected Avery to laugh again but she looked serious. I hoped she wasn't mad at me. "I'm glad you told me about all this," Avery said.

"Me too," I said. Mostly I was relieved because she didn't seem to think I was weird or awful. "Promise you won't tell anyone else? Not Brenna or Callie or anyone?"

"I promise," Avery said.

"Thanks," I said.

"I pinky swear!" she said. "Remember that?" I nodded. When I was younger, I used to always pinky swear with Heidi when things were important. Avery made a fist and held it up toward me, her pinky extended and curved into a little hook. I made a hook with my pinky and locked my finger with hers.

"Pinky swear," I said.

A few minutes later Lori brought us hot chocolate with marshmallows floating on the top. I could see the steam rising and I blew hard into the mug to cool it off. The hot chocolate sloshed up against the sides. Lori said she had called Mom and Simon, and Simon would be coming over to pick me up after dinner. I nodded and took a sip of my hot chocolate. Even though I had tried to cool it off, it still burned a little.

chapterfourteen

S chool got really hard all of a sudden, which is what happens right before winter vacation. Well, not for Charlie, since he's just in kindergarten. Everything stayed the same for him. I had final exams in every single class, except for art and gym. Avery complained about all the studying they expected us to do, but I was sort of glad about it. I didn't have to talk to Mom or Simon, because I had so many tests to study for, and I didn't have to think about how strange and terrible everything was, because I was busy thinking about all the work I had to do.

Our algebra exam was first. I'm a pretty fast test-taker overall, so I usually have time to go over my answers and make sure everything is right. I went over the algebra exam and I still had time left over. I looked around the room. Everyone was still bent over their desks. I saw our teacher, Mrs. Simmons, at the front of the room. She caught my eye, and I looked down quickly because I didn't want her to think I was looking around the room to try to cheat. I've never cheated on a test. Besides, math is one of my best subjects, and I thought I'd done pretty well, so there wouldn't have been any reason for me to cheat.

There were still ten minutes before the exam period
was over. You're not allowed to leave the room until the
bell rings and all the exams are collected. I didn't feel like
going over my test a third time so I just sat there waiting.
I wondered what would happen if I just opened my mouth
and screamed. Right there in the middle of class. It would
be so easy to do. No one was stopping me. I wondered what
it would sound like. I don't think I've ever just opened my
mouth and screamed like that. Mom once screamed when
she saw a mouse in our kitchen in Baltimore. Simon called
an exterminator, who flashed a light underneath the fridge
and then set up glue traps around the kitchen in case there
were any more mice. For the rest of the week, Mom and I
avoided the kitchen as much as we could.

If I screamed in the middle of the classroom, I could
pretend I'd seen a mouse. I wondered if everyone would
start laughing at me or if I would get in trouble. Maybe they
wouldn't believe me about the mouse and they would think I
was sick, like mentally ill or something, and Mrs. Simmons
would send me to the nurse's office. Maybe Mrs. Simmons
wouldn't make the class finish the test because they would
all be so worried about me.

I had been feeling crazy lately, but of course I didn't do
it. I guess I wasn't really crazy after all. Instead I just sat
there with my lips pressed together. The room was quiet
except for the pencils moving across the papers. I heard the
girl next to me erase something, and then brush her hand
across the page to get rid of the bits of eraser.

Finally the bell rang. Mrs. Simmons made us all stay

seated and she walked around the room collecting our exams, and then Avery and I headed over to our lockers. One of the things I like about Avery is that she isn't one of those people who finishes a test and then talks about every single question that was on it and insists on comparing answers. Brenna and Callie, on the other hand, can't help but talk about tests when they're over. It's like they want to relive the whole experience. We had a history exam the next day. Even though we're in different classes, the entire eighth grade had the same textbook and was getting the same exam, so we decided to study together. Avery and I said we would meet Brenna and Callie at Brenna's house. That way the two of them could talk all they wanted about the algebra exam on the way over, and the two of us wouldn't have to hear it.

"I want to pick up some snacks on the way to Brenna's," Avery said. "There's never anything good to eat in her house. Is that all right?"

"Sure," I said. "Then they'll have extra time to talk all about the exam."

Avery rolled her eyes. "I *so* don't want to talk about that exam," she said. "It was totally impossible. It was like Mrs. Simmons expected us to be human calculators or something. I mean, there were like a million questions and we only had one hour. I didn't even have time to finish!"

I didn't tell her that I had actually finished the test early. I just nodded.

"So, do you want to use my phone?" Avery asked.

"Yes," I said.

Avery opened her bag and pulled out her cell phone,

which is bright pink. I have the same phone, except that mine is silver. I pressed the button to turn it on. Avery had programmed her phone so when it turns on, it plays a song from that show she likes. It's sort of annoying because it takes longer for her phone to turn on and for the screen to clear so you can dial, but of course I've never said that to Avery. I waited for the song to end so I could call Samantha.

It was this thing we did now. Avery let me use her cell phone to call Samantha, just in case Mom and Simon were monitoring my cell phone bill for phone calls to Samantha. At first I was worried that Avery would get in trouble because there would be extra minutes on her cell phone bill, but Avery said her dad had signed up for a family plan with a zillion minutes, and her parents didn't keep track of how many she used, or who she was calling.

I dialed Samantha's number. Avery had offered to program it into her phone, but I knew it by heart so I didn't need her to program it in. Besides, it would have been weird for Avery to have Samantha's phone number stored in her phone. I didn't even have Samantha's number programmed into *my* phone, in case Mom or Simon went snooping around. I didn't want Avery to be closer to Samantha in that way. I didn't want her to be able to call Samantha even when I wasn't around.

Avery had pulled her iPod out of her bag, and now she had the white earphones stuck in her ears. I pressed the phone against my ear. Samantha answered after the third ring.

"Hey," she said.

"Hey, it's Leah," I said.

"I know," she said. "I saw on the caller ID." It was sort of strange how Samantha recognized me even though I was calling from someone else's phone. "It's so cool you just called. I have to tell you something."

"What?"

"Well, you know Henry and Andrew?"

"From the Lyon's Sibling Registry?"

"Yeah," she said. "Well, they just moved to California with their moms."

"Aren't they brothers?"

"Yup," she said. "Twins. They have two moms. Anyway, they just moved to California. So we were e-mailing back and forth, and they're gonna come back east for a donor sibling reunion. We haven't worked out exactly where it's going to be, but it's gonna be during spring break, I think the third weekend in March. I spoke to Tate, and he's gonna come too, with his parents."

I felt something drop inside me. Samantha sounded so excited to see the boys. I guess I understood. I mean, they were her brothers just the same as I was her sister. But somehow it made me feel like I didn't count anymore. Maybe it was just because they would be all together, and I wouldn't get to be there. Samantha, Henry, Andrew, and Tate all had parents who understood about the Lyon's Sibling Registry. Not like my parents. Mom and I had barely spoken about it since that first time. Mostly she and Simon talked about how important our family was—she and Simon and Charlie and me. Like it was all enough. Like Samantha and the boys didn't matter at all.

Like if we didn't talk about them, they would just go away.

"Anyway," Samantha continued, "it's still a few months away, so maybe your parents will get used to all this by then and you all can come."

"I don't know," I said.

"Oh, come on," Samantha said. "We can't have a reunion without you! I'd be the only girl. I totally need my sister!"

I felt better when she said that. Maybe there would be a way to work it all out. I had three whole months to get Mom and Simon to understand everything about the Lyon's Sibling Registry. And if that didn't work, I had three months to think of an excuse to go to Pennsylvania without them.

When I got to Brenna's, I pulled my Palm Pilot out of my bag. It used to be Simon's, but he got a new one, so he gave the old one to me. Charlie wanted it because he likes the beeping sounds it makes when you set the alarm. But I told Simon I needed it for school, which is more important than Charlie having it as a toy. Simon agreed and he deleted all his work stuff. I plugged in things like homework assignments, my friends' birthdays, and other important dates so I wouldn't forget them. It was a lot more fun to use than the day planner that Mom had given me in the fall.

Avery had torn open a bag of Doritos and was looking through a gossip magazine that she'd bought at the deli. Brenna and Callie went into the kitchen to get us all sodas. Brenna had only diet soda at her house, which I hate, but I'd been so distracted on the phone with Samantha that I had forgotten to buy regular soda when Avery and I were buying snacks. I wasn't that thirsty, so it didn't matter anyway. I turned on my Palm Pilot and clicked the arrow to go forward until March, and I counted to the third weekend. Then I saw it: ROSS FAMILY REUNION. Simon's big family reunion, when we all went back to Baltimore and everyone even remotely related to Simon showed up.

There was no way I would get to see Samantha and the boys that weekend. I wasn't even related to the Ross family, but Mom and Simon would make me go to the reunion for sure.

"All right," Brenna said as she came back into the room. She put the soda on little coasters on the coffee table. "Let's get this over with."

"Please, not yet," Avery said. "I'm just at the good part." She held up the magazine and pointed to a picture in the center of the page. "You guys think Chase is so great, but really, have you ever seen anyone as cute as Brody Hudson? I just love his show. Don't you?"

"It's all right," Brenna said.

"Did you see it last night?" Avery asked.

"No," Brenna said. "I was studying."

"Oh, I took a break to watch it, and it was awesome," Avery said.

"I watched it on the phone with Ian last night," Callie said. "But he thinks the writing on the show isn't really that good anymore. You know, the head writer left or something, so Ian says the show might even be canceled."

"Oh, I'm gonna cry," Avery said. "They totally cannot cancel it." I thought it was strange the things that made Avery want to cry. Callie shrugged.

Brenna heaved our history textbook onto the table. "Come on, you guys," she said. "Hey, Callie, Megan must have used this book last year. How'd she say the exam was?"

Callie shrugged. "I wouldn't know," she said.

"Should we call her?" Brenna asked. "You know, sometimes teachers give the same exam two years in a row. Maybe she'll remember some of the questions."

"I don't think we should call her," Callie said.

"I still think you guys should just make up," Avery said.

"I told you," Callie said. "We can't just make up. It's not like that at all."

There was a silence for a couple of seconds. Avery was looking at Callie. I could tell she didn't understand why it had to be so hard. I looked back down at my Palm Pilot and pressed the button to turn it off. "Well," Avery said finally, "the study outline Chase made is in my bag. So I guess it doesn't matter now anyway."

"Oh, thank goodness for Chase," Brenna said. "Of course he made a study outline."

"I'm sure he got a higher grade than Megan anyway," Callie said. She had been sitting forward on the couch, but now she sat back like she was relaxed.

"Probably," Avery said. "He's made an outline for practically every class he's ever taken." She rolled up her magazine and reached toward her backpack. The bag of Doritos that was on her lap pitched forward.

"Don't get the chips everywhere," Brenna said. "My mom'll kill me."

"I'll clean it up," Avery said.

"But I wanted some of those," Callie said.

"Well, there aren't any left in the bag," Avery said. "But you know, ten-second rule. You can eat them off the floor."

"That's gross," Brenna said. "Just throw them away."

"But there's nothing else to snack on here," Callie said.

"Sorry," Brenna said. "I told you we should have just gone to Avery's."

"Oh, no," Avery said. "Then you guys would just be all obsessed with Chase, and we wouldn't get anything done."

"We would not," Brenna said.

"Whatever," Avery said. "He's holed up in his room studying anyway. *I'm* barely allowed to talk to him."

"Can we just get started?" Brenna said. "You guys can order a pizza or something if you want."

"You see?" Avery said. "I knew the only reason you wanted to go to my house was to see Chase!"

"It's just that we're already here," Brenna said. "And we really should get started on this."

"So are we gonna order pizza or what?" Callie asked.

"I'm not hungry," Brenna said.

Avery rolled her eyes. "I'll have a slice. What about you, Leah? You're so quiet. Are you nervous about the exam?"

I shrugged. Avery looked worried about me for a second, but I knew it was only because she thought I was scared about the test. "We'll start studying as soon as we order, I promise," she said.

I remembered eating pizza with Samantha—pepperoni, because that was her favorite. I hated the idea of Samantha being with the boys without me. I didn't understand how Callie seemed to forget all about Megan so quickly. It just seemed too easy for sisters to disappear.

Suddenly I didn't want to be around anyone. I just wanted to be alone. "It's okay," I said. "I think I might just go study at home. I'm not really feeling well."

"Are you sure?" Avery asked. I nodded. If I were home, I could study and stop thinking about Samantha so much. I could just focus on my history exam and not think about anyone else. I put my Palm Pilot back into my bag and zipped it up. "Call me later," Avery said.

"I will," I said. I stood up and pulled my bag over my shoulder. "Sorry, guys," I said. "I'll see you tomorrow."

chapterfifteen

A couple weeks later Chase found out that he didn't get into Yale. Avery and her family were supposed to go skiing over Christmas break, but Mr. Monahan canceled the trip. He said it was because he couldn't get away from work, but Avery said that it was really because of Yale.

Simon and Mom took Charlie and me back to Baltimore for a long weekend over New Year's so we could visit some of our old friends and also Simon's parents. They pinched Charlie's and my cheeks as soon as we walked in the door. "Oh, you've gotten so much bigger!" Simon's mother said. I'm supposed to call her Grandma Diane, like Charlie does. It always sounds weird to me, since she wasn't my grandmother until I was almost eight years old.

"I've grown a lot," Charlie said, which wasn't really true.

"Yes, you have," Grandma Diane agreed. "And you, too, Leah." She put her arm around me and squeezed me in. She smelled kind of funny, like mothballs and hair spray. I stifled a cough. "I've been cooking for you all day," she said.

"Oh, no," Simon said. "What's for dinner, Ma?"

"It's a surprise," Simon's mother said.

"Watch out for Grandma's surprises, kids," Simon said.

"She used to make me eat liverwurst." I almost started to gag. I put my hand to my mouth, and Simon must have noticed because he came over to me and put his hand on my shoulder. "I know, Leah, it's awful. I used to tell her I didn't want to have to eat anything with the word 'worst' in it!"

I shrugged my shoulder, so Simon moved his hand. "Oh, you," Simon's mother told him. "Leave me alone. I didn't make liverwurst this time, but it's good for you, just so you know."

I followed everyone into the living room because I had to. Simon's parents had invited a few people over for dinner, and Mom and Simon had invited a couple of their friends. Mom had invited my old friend Heidi and her mother, but they had gone away for the weekend, and I was secretly glad. I didn't feel like seeing Heidi. Everything that was going on was making me feel different from everybody else. Mom asked if there was anyone else I wanted to invite, but I told her no. "Everyone's probably on vacation," I said. Besides, the house was pretty full with the people Mom, Simon, and Simon's parents had invited. Simon's sister, Amy, her husband, and their kids were there. Amy had just had a new baby, and Mom and Simon were all excited to meet it, even though it didn't do much except scream and sleep. There weren't as many people at dinner as there usually are at the family reunion, but it seemed like enough to me. I asked Mom if it meant we didn't have to go to the reunion in March. "Of course we have to go," Mom said. "It's a tradition. Besides, you love going."

"No, I don't," I told her.

"What's going on, Leah?"

"Nothing," I said. "Never mind."

"Oh, Leah, this new attitude of yours has to change," Mom said.

"Whatever," I said. Mom ignored me and walked into the kitchen to help Simon's mother put the finishing touches on dinner.

Luckily, we didn't stay with Simon's parents. We stayed at a hotel instead, which was kind of strange since our old house was so close by. We even drove past the house, but we didn't go inside. The new owners had put different-colored curtains in all the windows. I looked at my old room and wondered what it looked like inside, but Mom and Simon wouldn't let us ring the doorbell. They said it wouldn't be right to intrude on the new owners like that. I didn't see what the big deal was, but since Mom and Simon didn't seem to understand anything I had to say, I didn't say anything about it.

I called Avery the day after we got back from Baltimore. "Finally!" she said. "I'm so glad you're back. Everyone is away except me. It's totally boring. You have to come over today."

"Are you sure?" I asked.

"Of course I'm sure," she said.

"I mean, does Chase need privacy or something?"

"Oh, you won't even see Chase," Avery said. "He doesn't ever come out of his room these days, unless he has to go to the bathroom or something. Lizzie came over the other day, and he wouldn't even come out of his room to talk to her."

"I thought they were still fighting," I said.

"Well, I guess Lizzie thought everything was fine with them since he's not going to Yale, but Chase is really upset. He won't talk to anyone, not even Lizzie. My dad was giving him a really hard time at first, banging on his door and all that. But now even he's given up trying to get Chase to talk to him. Lizzie was hysterically crying when she left the house the other day. My mom had to drive her home because she was crying so hard. Chase told me once that she could be dramatic."

"Wow," I said. "Doesn't sound like it's been that boring."

"So it's not exactly boring," Avery said. "But it's been really lonely. I mean, the only person in my house who speaks to me is my mom."

I knew what she meant about feeling lonely. The only person in my family that I wasn't mad at was Charlie. I didn't even have Samantha to talk to, and not just because I didn't have Avery's cell phone when I was in Baltimore. Samantha's mom had been picked to be a faculty advisor on a college trip to Paris. Samantha got to go with her, but her cell phone didn't work in France. "I just need to tell my mom and I'll come over," I told Avery.

"Hurry up," she said.

It was pretty warm outside. Simon said it was called January thaw and that it happened every year, but I couldn't remember it ever being so warm in January. I was wearing my winter jacket, but I took it off and folded it over my arm.

Avery's house is set back from the road. There's a

cobblestone path leading up to the front door, which is really old-fashioned looking. It always makes me think there should be a horse and buggy parked in the driveway, even though the inside of the house is really modern and they have all sorts of gadgets. I rang the doorbell and heard Avery shrieking inside. She flung open the door. "Hey!" she cried, throwing her arms around me. "It's so good to see you! How are you?"

"Fine," I said. "Hot, actually. It's really warm out."

"Do you want a drink to cool off? We have tons of stuff—soda, water, juice. What do you want?"

"What kind of juice do you have?" I asked.

"I'm not sure," Avery said. "But go take whatever you want." She waved me toward the kitchen. "I have to get something to show you."

"All right," I said. "Do you want anything?" Avery shook her head. I headed into the kitchen and pulled open the refrigerator door. Avery called after me, but I couldn't understand what she was saying. "What?" I called back.

"A Coke," she shouted louder. "Can you bring me a Coke?"

"Sure," I shouted back.

"Shut up," Chase called from upstairs, and I felt my cheeks flush. I had screwed up with Chase again.

"Shut up yourself," Avery called back.

I heard a door open upstairs, and then heavy footsteps. I took a deep breath and pulled out a mini carton of orange juice—the kind with the straw attached that Charlie brings to school in his lunch box—along with a can of Coke for

Avery. I shut the door and walked slowly back toward the front hall. Chase was leaning over the railing and I stepped back so he wouldn't be able to see me. "Jeez, Avery, can't you keep it down so the rest of us can have some peace and quiet?"

"What are you talking about? There's no 'rest of us.' Mom's out, Dad's at work. It's just you upstairs hiding out. And it's not like I'm playing the drums or something down here. Leah just got here. We were just saying hello. We're probably gonna go out soon anyway."

"Leah's here?"

"Duh," Avery said. "What'd you think—that I was talking to myself? Of course she's here. And she must think you're a real jerk too, since you always act like one whenever she's around."

"Yeah," Chase said. I stood in the doorway, waiting to hear him walk away before I stepped out. "Where is she?" he asked.

"You probably scared her away," Avery said.

"Leah," Chase said. "It's all right to come out. I won't bite."

"You could have fooled me," Avery said.

I stepped forward into the front hall. "I'm right here," I said.

"Sorry about that," Chase said. "I didn't know it was you."

"It's okay," I said. "I'm sorry if I was too loud."

"Don't apologize to him," Avery said.

"Right," Chase said, starting down the stairs. "Don't

apologize to me. I was a total jerk, and you're a guest."

"Uh-huh," Avery said. "She's a guest. Mom would have a fit if she heard you being rude to a guest. You know she's always saying how she doesn't care how we act in private, but we have to hold it together in front of guests."

"I get it, Avery," Chase said. "I think Leah will forgive me. It's not like it was one of Dad's partners and now the world is about to end. Right, Leah?"

"Yes, it's fine, really," I said. I smiled to show him that I meant it. Chase had his elbows propped up on the railing, and he was leaning down so his hair fell forward and I couldn't see his eyes. He was wearing a white shirt with the sleeves torn off, so the edges were frayed, and a pair of those pants that doctors wear, I think they're called scrubs—they were blue with a drawstring front. I wondered where Chase had gotten them since neither of his parents were doctors. I'd never seen him in a sleeveless shirt before, and I could see the muscles in his arms.

"Whatever," Avery said. "Leah, I have to get something to show you." I turned away from Chase to look at her. She started up the stairs. "Behave yourself, Chase," she said as she passed him. Chase swatted at her and walked down toward me.

"I guess Avery told you everything that happened," Chase said, and I shrugged. "Quite a Christmas break, huh?"

"I'm sort of looking forward to going back to school," I told him.

"Yeah, me too. Isn't that crazy?" Chase asked. He swept his bangs back from his forehead so his hair kind of stuck up in the front. It made him look younger. "It's just been so hard around here."

"I'm sorry about Yale," I said.

"Yeah, well, maybe it wasn't meant to be." Chase held out his hand toward me, and I wasn't sure what I was supposed to do. Besides, I was still holding the juice and soda. Then he said, "Can I have one of those?"

"Oh, sure," I said, holding the juice and soda out. "Which one?"

"I don't care," he said. I handed him the orange juice since the Coke was really for Avery. I didn't want her to get mad at Chase for drinking it, even though there was plenty more in the fridge. "Thanks," Chase said. He tore the straw off the side and banged it against the carton so the wrapper would come off. I watched him pierce the top of the carton with the tip of the straw and take a long gulp. I stood there looking at him like an idiot because I wasn't sure what I was supposed to say. Avery was taking a long time getting whatever it was that she wanted to show me. Chase drank the whole carton of orange juice without even stopping for a breath. There was a slurping sound when he finished it, and he squeezed the carton in his fist. "Did Avery tell you my father's theory?" he asked.

"Theory about what?"

"About Yale," he said. I shook my head. "Oh, this is a good one," he said. "My father's theory is that the admissions committee could tell that my heart wasn't in it, that I really didn't want to go to Yale. Even though I worked my butt off for the last three and a half years in high school and got almost a perfect score on the SATs. He thinks my application just smelled wrong, and that's why they weren't interested in me. It couldn't have anything to do with the fact that there are a million other kids just like me applying to Yale."

"I'm sorry," I said.

"Yeah, me too," Chase said. "You know, he's wrong about me, too. I mean, I wanted to get into Yale. I really did. It meant so much to him and all of that. But when the envelope came—it was a thin envelope, not a fat one—and I just knew that I didn't get in, he was acting like he was the one who was rejected and not me. I kept telling him, 'You know, there are other schools out there. I'll probably still get into some Ivy League school.' But for him there's only one school."

"Maybe you'll get into a school that's even better than Yale," I said.

"Yeah," Chase said. "I told him that, too. He got rejected from Harvard when he applied, so I told him, maybe I'll be the one to get into Harvard."

"That'd show him, right?"

"Yeah, maybe," he said. "Listen, I'm sorry to unload all of this on you. All my friends are so weird about college right now, and I haven't really talked to anyone about this. But you're not like Avery's other friends—they're nice girls, but they just come here and giggle, you know?"

"I guess," I said, shrugging.

"Sorry," he said. "I know they're your friends too, right?"

"Yes, they are," I said.

"You really are an old soul," Chase said, and I shrugged

again. "It's very cool," he continued. "You're easy to talk to. But I shouldn't complain to you. Anyway, it's not so bad, and I know you're going through some really bad stuff with your family."

"You know?" I asked. I felt my palms getting slippery and I gripped the can of soda tighter.

"Yeah," Chase said. "And I want you to know that I think you're really brave. It's cool, you know."

"It's not so cool," I said stepping backward a little.

Chase stepped forward and put his hand on my shoulder. "That's not what I meant," he said.

Suddenly I felt like we were standing too close, and I wanted to get away. "Can you tell Avery that I had to go?" I asked.

"Leah, don't go," he said. "I'm sorry. I shouldn't have said anything."

At that moment Avery came running down the stairs waving something in her hand. "Leah!" she said. "Look at this!"

"I gotta go," I said. I turned around and headed toward the door.

"Leah, I'm sorry," Chase said again, but I didn't turn around. I pulled open the front door. Behind me I could hear Avery asking Chase what had happened.

"What did you say this time?" she asked. I closed the door before I could hear what he said, and I ran down the cobblestone path. I knew Avery would probably follow me and I didn't want to talk to her, but the cobblestones were pretty bumpy and it was hard to run. I had almost made it to the sidewalk when I tripped and fell. I was still holding the can of Coke, but it slipped out of my hand. It must have landed on something sharp because it burst open and the soda sprayed out. "Leah!" Avery said. "Are you all right?"

I stood up and wiped the soda off my shirt. My face was wet too, partly from crying and partly from the soda. "Just leave me alone," I said, turning away from her. I started walking again, but this time I was more careful. I didn't feel steady on my feet anymore.

"Leah, please," Avery said. "I know you think I told Chase about your family, but I didn't. I swear."

I spun back around. "Then how does he know? Did you tell Brenna or Callie and one of them told him?"

"No," she said. "I promised that I wouldn't say anything, and I didn't. I don't know how he knows. I guess my mom told him."

We stood there staring at each other, like those contests I used to have with Heidi when I was little—we'd stare at each other and wait to see who blinked first. I realized that I believed Avery about not telling Chase, but I couldn't help but be mad. I hated people knowing things about me. Everything seemed out of control. "I knew I should never tell anyone about this," I said finally.

"But I'm glad you told me," Avery said. "Come back inside, please. You have soda in your hair." She started to step toward me, but I shook my head.

"I can't go back in there," I said.

"Why? Because of Chase?" I nodded. "Listen, Leah," Avery said, "you really worry too much about what other

people think. You don't have to cry. It's really no big deal."
She always said things weren't a big deal, and I was jealous
of her for thinking that way about everything. I wanted to
be more like her. The only time she ever talked about crying was when she couldn't watch her favorite stars on TV
anymore. But I also wished she could understand that everything with my family was a big deal—a very big deal—to me.
Avery never really thought about things being a big deal to
other people.

"You just don't understand," I told her.

"You know, you're not the only one with bad stuff," Avery
said. "You think it's so easy for me to be Chase Monahan's
sister? My dad keeps going on and on about how it would
have meant so much to him to have a child of his go to Yale,
and now he won't. It's like I don't even exist. He doesn't even
ask to see my report card. And by the way, I got an A-minus
on that math exam. Can you believe it? It's like a miracle
because I didn't even finish the test. That's what I wanted
to show you. My dad didn't care because it's not an A, and
besides I'll never be as good as Chase."

I know it sounds stupid and shallow, but I hadn't ever
really thought about Avery having problems. She was popular
and beautiful, and nothing ever really seemed to bother her. I'd
never even seen her hair look messy. Even when it was windy
out, her hair always seemed to fall the right way. "I don't know
what to say," I said. "I mean, you *are* as good as Chase."

"Not to my dad I'm not," Avery said. "But it's okay. My
point is, everyone has something that makes them feel bad
about themselves. Like Brenna's so obsessed with what she

eats so she doesn't end up like her mother, and Callie won't invite anyone over to her place because she lives in a small apartment and they don't have a lot of money."

"I didn't know that," I said.

"But if you did, would you like them any less? If Brenna gained ten pounds or if Callie's family had to move to an even smaller apartment, would you stop being their friend?"

"No, of course not," I said.

"You see?" she said. "None of it matters that much, and no one would stop liking you, either. I know that Brenna and Callie wouldn't change their minds about you if they knew. And Chase still likes you. He says you're the only one of my friends he actually likes hanging out with. But you don't give anyone any credit. You're so busy worrying what they're going to think."

"I'm not even sure what to think about it myself," I said.

"Just come back inside, please," Avery said. "Don't run away again."

"I don't run away."

"Yeah, you do. You ran over here when your mom found out, and then you ran away from Brenna's house when we were studying—I don't even know why. And now you were just running again."

I wiped my eyes with the back of my hand. My face felt sticky. I felt like I could start crying again.

"Come on," Avery said. She held her hand out to me. "Will you please come inside? You can borrow a shirt since yours is all wet. I really want to get out of the house. It's so warm outside, we could even get ice cream. We should get it today before it starts to be freezing again."

I took Avery's hand, and she squeezed mine and then pulled me toward the house. We went inside and I changed my shirt and washed my face, and then we did end up going out for ice cream. We sat in the same booth we had been in with Charlie and Callie, where I had been so worried about Callie reading my palm in case I had a bad family line. It seemed like a long time ago.

On the way home I thought a lot about what Avery had said about running away and not giving anyone any credit. I wondered if that was true about Mom and Simon, too. I hadn't really ever tried to explain to them everything about Samantha, and I hadn't told them anything about the sibling reunion in March. When I had asked Mom about the Ross family reunion, I hadn't told her why I didn't want to go. But maybe if I really explained it all, she would understand. Maybe I just had to stop being scared of telling people what I was thinking. I decided that I would ask Mom about going to Samantha's in March.

chaptersixteen

On my way home from ice cream with Avery, I decided exactly what I would say to Mom. I went over my conversation again and again in my head so I would remember what to say. We would sit down in my room and for once Charlie wouldn't come in and bother us. I would be very calm and I wouldn't cry or yell at all. I would explain how I'd first discovered the Lyon's Sibling Registry, and how awful it was when I saw it because I didn't want to hurt her feelings or get in trouble for using the credit card. But I'd decided that I had to sign up because I thought about how Charlie and I were half siblings. I loved Charlie so much— and if I had other half siblings, I wanted to know them, too. I would tell Mom how I had gotten to know Samantha. At first it was just over the phone and a few e-mails, and then Avery and Chase told me they were going to Haverford and it was like a sign that I was supposed to meet Samantha in person. I would say how important Samantha was to me now, and how much I wanted to meet Andrew, Tate, and Henry. And in my head, when I was all done, Mom would be crying a little but also smiling, and she would hug me and say that she understood that I needed to miss the Ross family reunion just this once.

When I got home, Charlie was in the den watching *The Lion King* for the millionth time. "Hey, Leah," he said. "Can you watch with me?"

"I have to talk to Mom first," I told him.

"But she's working," Charlie said.

"I'll be back in a little bit," I said.

I walked back toward the kitchen. Mom was sitting in her little office. She had gotten a letter back from her editor about her book, and her editor had said she needed to tweak some things and add a chapter, so I knew she had to be working on that. Mom hates to be interrupted when she's writing. It's like she gets into a writing groove, and if we bother her, she's afraid she won't be able to get back into it. But I had finally worked up the courage to talk to Mom, and I had it all planned in my head. I wanted to talk to her as soon as possible, before I chickened out or forgot everything I wanted to say. I leaned against the side of the doorway. "Hey, Mom," I said. "Can we talk a minute?"

"Oh, Leah, I didn't know you were home."

"I just got home," I said. "I'm sorry to bother you. I just wanted to talk to you about something."

"Well, I can take a break for a minute," Mom said.

I took a deep breath. For some reason, I thought it would be easier to talk to Mom if I were sitting down, but the only chair in Mom's office is her desk chair and she was already sitting on it. There's a small filing cabinet across from the desk. It had papers piled on top, so I picked them up and sat down on top of the cabinet. I could feel my heart begin to beat a little faster. I closed my eyes for a second and tried to calm down and remember what I wanted to say, but all of a sudden it was all jumbled up. I opened my eyes and Mom was staring at me. Her eyebrows were furrowed a little bit, which made the skin between her eyes bunch up and wrinkle. It's the face she makes when she's starting to get worried. "What's going on?" she asked.

"You know the Ross family reunion in March?" I asked.

"Yes, of course," Mom said. "What about it?"

"Well, the thing is . . . actually . . . Do you remember Samantha? She's the girl from the Lyon's Sibling Registry?"

"Of course I remember," Mom said.

"The thing is, she's planning a donor sibling reunion that same weekend. I'd get to see her, and meet my three half brothers."

"Oh, Leah, do we have to do this now? I have about thirty minutes before your brother gets bored of his video and wants something to eat, and I'm in the middle of this chapter."

"It's just . . . I know you're busy. But, Mom, this is important."

"You're coming with us in March," Mom said. "That is not negotiable."

"But, Mom, you're not . . . You don't understand." I was fumbling over my words. I'd started the wrong way because I was nervous. I shouldn't have told her right away that the reunions were the same weekend. I should have started with how much I loved Charlie, and how that was connected to my other half siblings. Maybe then she would have understood. Mom had stopped looking worried and now she just looked impatient. I could tell she wanted me to leave her alone so she could go back to writing.

"Leah," Mom said. "I can't deal with this now. You are a member of this family—the family right here in this house. Simon might not be your biological father, but he is your father. He's been there at all your school events, he has worried about you, he has supported you, he's home for dinner every night with you. That's what makes someone family. Maybe you don't understand that right now, but one day you will." I started to interrupt, but Mom held up her hand. "No, Leah, the Ross reunion is something we do, as a family, every year. Everyone in Simon's family will be there, and that includes you. You can't just suddenly decide you don't feel like going."

"But it's not that I suddenly don't want to go."

"Good, because you're going," Mom said.

"Stop it and listen to me for a second! It's not that I don't feel like going. You know I usually go, and I hang out with all the people in Simon's family like I'm supposed to. And it's not my fault that everything is on the same weekend. But I've gone to Simon's reunion every year, and besides we just saw Simon's family. I've never had the chance to hang out with my other siblings before."

"They're not as important as your family," Mom said.

"They are my family!" I cried.

"Oh, Leah," Mom said. "Please, not this again."

"They are, no matter what you say. And just because you don't think something is important doesn't mean it isn't important to me. You're just not listening to me."

"I am listening to you," Mom said. "You're not listening to me. I'm the grown-up. I know what's best. You can't pretend not to be a part of this family. Now I'm in the middle of a chapter, Leah, so we can talk more about this later."

"But, Mom, it's not fair!"

Of course that was the absolute wrong thing to say to Mom. "Don't start with what is not fair," she said. "You don't know what it means to have an unfair life. There are people in this world who deal with terrible things every day. But you have two parents who adore you and who take care of you, you have a brother who worships you, you have a roof over your head, you're healthy, you go to a wonderful school, you have friends. Do you need me to keep going?" I shook my head. I could tell Mom would never listen to me. Samantha would be so disappointed, and I wouldn't get to meet the boys. "All right, then," Mom said. She turned back to her computer.

I stood up. I knew I was going to start crying and Mom wouldn't care. I was still holding Mom's papers, but instead of putting them back on top of the cabinet, I held them up and then opened up my hands so they fluttered to the floor.

Mom turned away from her computer and saw the mess on the floor. "That's just great, Leah," she said, looking back and forth from the floor to me. "You expect me to let you make grown-up decisions, and then you act immature when you don't get your way. Pick those up and put them back where you found them."

"No," I said.

"Leah, I've had about enough of this," Mom said.

"I've had enough too," I said. I left the papers where they were, scattered on the floor of Mom's little office. She would have to clean them up herself. I pounded my way through the kitchen into the front hall.

"Hey, Leah," Charlie called as I passed by the den. I knew he wanted me to watch the video with him, but I was sick of trying to be anyone's sister. It was like I was always failing. "Leah!" Charlie called again. "Hey, Dudette!"

He started laughing at his own joke, his deep-throated laugh that makes him sound much older than five years old, the one that Mom says sounds like her father. He got up to chase after me, stumbling because he was still laughing, but I held my hand out toward him. "Leave me alone," I said.

I started up the stairs. If Avery could have seen me, maybe she would have said I was running away again. But I didn't care. Charlie had stopped laughing. He was still following me. "Leah, what's the matter?" he said.

I spun around. "I said leave me alone!"

"Are you crying?" Charlie asked, his voice catching a little like he was about to start crying too. He always cries when he sees me crying. Usually I try not to cry in front of him because it makes him so upset. But right then I didn't care about Charlie.

"Get away from me!" I screamed at him. "I hate you! I hate all of you!" I ran up the stairs as Charlie started to wail. I heard Mom running toward the front hall. When I got to my room, I slammed the door as hard as I could. Then I pushed in the little button on the doorknob so it would lock and Charlie wouldn't be able to come in. I flopped down on my bed and buried my face in my pillow. The pillow was so soft. It had been Mom's pillow from when she was a little girl, and over the years it had lost a lot of its fluff. But it was a great pillow to burrow into and I pressed my face in harder.

It was hard to breathe but I didn't care. A few seconds later I heard Mom's footsteps in the hallway. She didn't even knock before she tried to come in. I could hear her at the door trying to turn the knob.

"Leah, open this door," Mom said. I turned so I was no longer facedown in the pillow, but I didn't answer and I didn't stand up to open the door. "Open this door," Mom said again.

I could hear Charlie whining next to her. "I didn't do anything. Why does Leah hate me?"

"All right, Leah," Mom said, talking louder so she could be sure I heard her through the door. "You stay in there and don't come out until you are ready to apologize to Charlie and apologize to me. Until then, I don't want to see you."

I put my face back in my pillow. I wished I didn't ever have to leave my room. I felt like throwing up, and I slipped my hand underneath my stomach and pressed against it. Even though my eyes were closed, it was like everything was spinning. My stomach hurt so much, but I didn't want to leave my room to go to the bathroom. I turned over and pulled my knees up to my chest.

I don't know how long I was lying there. It seemed like a really long time. My stomach was killing me, so finally I had to get up to go to the bathroom. I still felt dizzy so I steadied myself against the wall and walked down the hall to the bathroom. I shut the door and I tried to focus on one thing—the robe hanging on the back of the door—so the room would stop spinning and I could see straight. I looked at the robe as I pulled down my pants and sat on the toilet.

I knew something had to be wrong with me. I clutched

my stomach in my arms and bent forward. That's when I saw the blood. There was so much of it. It had seeped through my underwear onto my jeans. I knew it had to be my period, but I wasn't used to it looking this way—dark, dark red and not at all rusty. I stood up and looked down at the toilet. The water was red from all the blood. This couldn't be what Mom had meant when she'd said my period would get heavier. It was so disgusting. There was so much blood I thought maybe I was hemorrhaging. I felt my heart beginning to pound again. I pulled at the toilet paper and pressed it against myself to try to staunch the bleeding, just like Mom did when Charlie cut his finger and needed stitches. "Mom!" I shouted. "Mom!"

Mom didn't answer. Either she didn't hear me or she was just ignoring me. I dropped the bloody toilet paper into the toilet and sucked in my breath. I held the air in the back of my throat for a few seconds, and then I opened my mouth and screamed as loud as I could. It seemed to go on forever and my ears were ringing. I screamed until my throat was raw and I didn't have any breath left. It was all so hard. There was so much blood and nothing was fair, no matter what Mom said.

Afterward it was very quiet, like the quiet that comes after a really bad storm. I swallowed and my throat hurt even more than my stomach. I ripped off another piece of toilet paper and wiped my face and blew my nose. Then I heard Charlie yelling. "Mom, Mom, come quick! Something's wrong with Leah!"

There were footsteps in the hall again and then the door swung open. I hated the door being open when my pants were around my ankles. Even though I still had my shirt on, I felt totally naked. "What's going on with you now?" Mom asked.

"I don't know," I said. "I'm bleeding so much. I've never seen it like this before."

Mom stepped forward and saw the blood on my pants. "Your period?" she asked, and I nodded. I was crying again and I gulped because it was hard to breathe and cry at the same time.

In an instant Mom's whole face softened. "It's okay," she said. "Really. My period was very heavy when I was your age. Don't worry. You're going to be fine. You just need to get cleaned up. Do you still have that box of pads I bought you?" I nodded.

"They're under the sink," I said. My voice came out like a whisper.

"All right," Mom said. She turned on the faucet in the bathtub. "I'm going to get you some clean underwear. Just take a bath and get cleaned up, okay?"

"Okay," I said.

I waited until the bathtub was mostly filled up before I got in. Mom had pulled the pads out from underneath the sink and put them on the shelf next to the tub, along with the clean underwear. The water between my legs was a little pink from the blood. After a little while I stood up and turned the shower on to wash everything off of me. It was the longest shower I had ever taken.

Mom was sitting on my bed when I got back to my room. "Better?" she asked.

"I guess," I said. "This pad feels kind of like a diaper."

"You'll get used to it," Mom said, and I nodded.

"I'm sorry I was so mean to Charlie," I said.

"I know," Mom said.

"I didn't mean it," I said.

"I know," she said. She was staring at me. Her eyes moved up and down and I pulled the robe tighter around me. "What?" I asked.

"It's just that you're growing up," Mom said. She shook her head like she almost didn't believe it. "I used to know everything about you."

"I'm thirteen," I said. "I don't think you're supposed to know everything about me anymore."

"I'm realizing that," Mom said. She wiped her eyes with one of her knuckles. "Oh, it's hard to be a parent. You know, you'll figure this out for yourself when you have children, but mostly I'm just winging this. I don't always know what I'm doing, and I don't always do the right thing. Maybe if my mother hadn't died, she would've been able to help me. Maybe she would have told me how you're supposed to act when your daughter starts growing up. I just don't know."

It was a little scary to hear Mom say she didn't know what she was doing. Part of me liked it better when she was more sure of herself. "I'm sorry," I said.

"No, I'm sorry," Mom said. "I guess I wasn't listening before. I'm listening now."

I sat down on the bed next to Mom. My stomach didn't hurt as much anymore. I just felt emptied out. "The thing with Samantha and the boys," I started, "it has nothing to do with you and Simon." I watched Mom's face to see if she was mad that I was bringing Samantha up again, but she just nodded. "You guys and Charlie are still the most important to me. But this donor sibling reunion . . . I just really want to be there. Don't you understand?"

Mom sighed. I thought about how strange and replaceable I felt when Samantha had first told me about the reunion. Maybe Mom felt left out too. After all, I had found siblings that she wasn't even related to. "I understand," she said. "But you know you have to go to the Ross reunion. You understand that, right? You just can't do that to Simon."

"But, Mom," I said.

"We can figure this out, Leah."

"How?"

"I was thinking about it while you were in the bath, and I thought maybe we could compromise. Baltimore isn't that far away from Philadelphia. Maybe I can call Samantha's mother and work out a way for them to come to the Ross reunion. After all, they're your family too."

"Do you mean it?"

"Well, I can't promise anything. I don't know if they'll all agree to come to Baltimore. But if they do, then why not? Simon's family is so enormous. A few more guests won't hurt anyone." Mom put her arm around my shoulder and I leaned into her. I started crying again, but it felt different this time.

"It's all right," Mom said. "I love you."

"I love you, too," I said.

"Yeah, I know," Mom said. It felt so good to be leaning up against her that I didn't even correct her.

chapterseventeen

It's amazing that some things really do work out. On the third Saturday in March, Simon drove us down to Baltimore. It was the same park we'd been to every year since Mom and Simon had met, but it looked different this time. Maybe it was because we had moved away and being in Baltimore didn't feel like being home anymore. Even though there were a few clouds swirling around, everything looked really bright and brand new.

"I hope it doesn't rain," Mom told Simon as we stepped out of the car. "It would destroy your mother's theory."

"What theory?" I asked.

"It's never rained at a Ross family reunion," Simon said. "Your grandmother thinks that's a sign that the family will always be lucky." I didn't really mind that he'd called his mother my grandmother. "What do you think, Chuck?" Simon asked.

"The clouds sort of look like polar bears," Charlie said.

"Polar bears? I don't think they have any polar bears in Baltimore," Simon said.

"But they have polar bears in Canada," Charlie said. "Real live ones, not just cloud ones. Can we go there?"

"To Canada?" Mom asked. Charlie nodded. "Not right

now," Mom said. "We just got to Baltimore."

"I didn't mean now," Charlie said. "I meant some other time, like maybe next week."

"Come over here, Chuck," Simon said, and he grabbed Charlie around the middle and hoisted him up onto his shoulders. The way Simon lifted Charlie up made it look like Charlie barely weighed anything at all. "You lead the way," Simon told him, and Charlie pointed to the picnic tables in the distance.

Mom came over and reached for my hand. I had spoken to Samantha from the car. Henry and Andrew and their mothers had flown into Philadelphia from California, and Tate and his mother had driven to Haverford. Anna Holland had rented a van, and they were all driving together from Pennsylvania to Baltimore. Samantha told me they were running a little late because there had been a long line at the car rental agency. She said there had been a mistake in the computer and the man at the agency had told them there weren't any vans left. But it all worked out and they would be there soon. In about a half hour I would see my half sister and meet my other half brothers. I gripped Mom's hand tightly, just like a little kid. Ever since I'd gotten my period and Mom had told me I was growing up, I was feeling younger than ever. "Nervous?" she asked.

"Yes," I said.

"Me too," Mom told me. "In fact, I'm *very* nervous. So is Simon. But we're excited for you too." She squeezed my hand a few times, the way she used to when I was little and we held hands a lot. She would squeeze my hand a few times, and then I would squeeze hers back the same number of times. I squeezed her hand back just like I used to do.

Simon's mother came running toward us. Every year she goes around with a camera hanging around her neck. She says her job at the reunion is to take pictures of everyone and "document the day for posterity." Simon always makes fun of her for it, because she's so busy taking pictures that she never sits down and just enjoys everyone being there. But I think taking pictures is Grandma Diane's way of enjoying the day. She orders copies of her favorite pictures, tapes them all up on poster boards, and decorates the trees around the park benches with all the posters she's made of the pictures from the past years. "Leah, Meredith, smile!" Simon's mother called as Mom and I walked over to her. We stopped in our tracks to pose for a picture.

"Hey, Ma," Simon called. "We just got here. There'll be plenty of time for pictures."

"Well, you know me, dear," she said. "I like to get started early." She stood on her tiptoes to hug Simon hello, and tugged at Charlie's legs.

"Hey, Grandma," Charlie called. "Do you see the polar bears in the sky?" Simon lifted him off his shoulders, and Grandma Diane bent down to Charlie's level. He pointed up to the clouds and I heard him tell her that Mom and Simon said maybe next week we would all go to Canada. Mom dropped my hand to say hello to all of the relatives. I knew I was supposed to say hello to everyone too, but I felt sort of funny because of everything that was about to happen.

I was sure they all knew about it. They all knew how Mom had gone to Lyon's Reproductive Services, and now they all knew that I was going to see Samantha and meet the rest of my donor siblings for the first time. I walked around the picnic tables and looked at the posters Simon's mother had made. There were pictures of me starting when I was seven years old, just before Mom and Simon got married. In one of them I was sitting on Simon's shoulders the way Charlie did now. Then there were a bunch of pictures of Charlie when he was a baby, and everyone holding him. Grandma Diane said he looked exactly like Simon did when he was a baby, but Mom told me she thought Charlie really took after her side of the family. "How're you doing, Leah?" Simon asked from behind me.

"Okay I guess," I said.

"All these pictures are really something, aren't they?" he asked.

"Yeah," I said.

"It's amazing to see how everyone has gotten older. I mean, look at this one." He pointed to the picture of me on his shoulders. "Do you even remember when I could pick you up like that?" I shrugged. "And now here you are," Simon continued. "You're a young woman." I felt my cheeks get hot. I hated thinking about how Simon knew I'd gotten my period. "I hope you have a good time today, Leah," he said. "You know, no matter what, your mom and I will always be here for you."

"I know that," I said. Mom had told me the same thing at least a dozen times in the last couple of months.

"Good," he said. "Now come say hello to everyone. Your aunt Amy was just asking about you."

I followed Simon over to his sister, Amy. The baby was almost four months old now. He could hold his head up, which he hadn't been able to do when we'd seen him over New Year's. Simon walked away from us to help his brother with the barbecue. "Do you want to hold him?" Amy asked me.

"Can I?" I asked.

"Of course," Amy said. "Here," she said, and she handed the baby to me. "Just rock him a little. He's less fussy when you're standing and rocking."

I leaned the baby up against my left arm and swayed back and forth. He grabbed at my hair and yanked it. "Whoa," I said. "He's really strong."

"That's why I always wear my hair back now," Amy said. She took a clip out of her pocket. "I always keep extras handy," she said. She stood behind me and gathered my hair together. "Come on, Asher, let go of your cousin's hair. Good boy." I heard a little click as Amy pressed the clip together. She turned my face in her hands. "Well, it's kind of a bumpy ponytail, but it looks all right," she said.

"Thanks," I said. I talked to Amy for a little while. For a baby, Asher got heavy pretty quickly, so I handed him back over.

"Wait until you have a baby," Amy told me. "You feel worn down and tired all the time, but you get major arm muscles from all the heavy lifting!"

"Omigod, Leah! Leah!" It was Samantha's voice. I spun around, and there she was running toward me. Suddenly

I remembered my bumpy ponytail. I didn't want to see Samantha and meet my brothers with a messed-up ponytail. I pulled Amy's clip out of my hair and shook my head so my hair fell back over my shoulders, and then I ran toward Samantha. We met in the middle, and spun around and around.

When we let go, everyone was looking at us. There was Anna Holland standing with a group of people that I knew had to be my donor half brothers and their mothers, and Mom and Simon, and Charlie, and all of the Ross relatives. I imagined all of Simon's relatives thinking how weird it was to have my donor siblings there at the reunion. But I smiled because no matter how strange everyone thought it was, Samantha was still my sister. It was like Avery said—I couldn't worry so much about what other people were thinking. Samantha introduced me to Henry, Andrew, and Tate. They looked like they did in the picture Samantha had shown me. Henry and Andrew both had brown hair and olive skin, like Samantha and me. Tate's hair was lighter and his skin was a little paler, but he had green eyes. Mom took Charlie by the hand and walked over with him and Simon to meet everyone.

Charlie clung to Mom, the way he did when he was feeling shy. Mom and I had tried to explain it to him—how I had been born before Mom met Simon, and how I had had a donor and not a daddy, and how there were some other kids with the same donor. Even though Charlie is really smart, it was still pretty hard for him to understand. Now Charlie was pressing his face into Mom's middle. I pulled at his arm.

"Hey, Charlie," I said. "Remember how you said you wanted to meet Samantha? Now you can!" He let go of Mom and grabbed on to my arm. "This is Charlie," I told Samantha. "And this is my sister, Samantha." I felt the words catch in my throat a little, and Charlie noticed it too.

"Are you going to cry?" he asked. His voice sounded shaky, like he was getting ready to cry in case I was about to.

"Don't worry," I told Charlie. "If I cry, it's just because I'm happy."

"You can't cry when you're happy," Charlie said.

Samantha's eyes started to look shiny, and she blinked a few times. "Sure you can," she said.

Charlie looked back and forth between Samantha and me. I could tell he was trying to figure everything out. Then he threw his head back and laughed his deep laugh. "That's the funniest thing I've ever heard," he said.

Simon's brother, Eric, yelled out that he had a bunch of hot dogs ready. "I want one! I want one!" Charlie yelled, and he raced over to the barbecue. Samantha and I followed behind him. I heard Amy tell Eric to put one of the hot dogs back on the barbecue and make it really burned.

"That's not good for you, dear," Grandma Diane told her.

"Nothing about hot dogs is good for you, Ma," Amy said.

Tate walked over to Samantha and me. "You know *all* these people?" he asked me.

I nodded. "They're sort of my family," I told him.

"So we get to eat the hot dogs?"

"Of course," I said. "They're making burgers, too. You can have anything you want."

"Oh, awesome," Tate said.

A few minutes later I was sitting at a picnic table eating hot dogs with Samantha, Henry, Andrew, and Tate. It was hard not to stare at them. I decided we all had the same eyes, sort of. We definitely looked similar. Maybe it was our foreheads or our chins. I fingered my cheekbones. "Are you okay?" Samantha asked.

"Absolutely," I said. I picked up the mustard and squirted some onto my hot dog, and then held the bottle out to Henry.

"No, thanks," he said. "I hate condiments of all kinds."

"Really?" I asked. "But I love condiments."

"I hate them too," Andrew said.

"I only like ketchup," Tate said.

"It's so weird that we're all related," I said.

"I know, it's crazy," Samantha said.

"I keep trying to figure out if we look alike," I said. "I can't believe we don't like the same condiments!"

"We all like hot dogs," Tate said, and I laughed.

"So this is the Hoffman-Ross family," Samantha said. She held out her hand and gestured toward all of the other picnic tables. "They make very tasty hot dogs."

"Well, it's the Ross family. My mom and I are the only Hoffman-Rosses."

"Oh, that's right," she said. "Well, they all seem nice. I told you it would work out."

"I know," I said. "I guess I shouldn't have worried so much."

"What were you worried about?" Andrew asked.

"I don't know really," I said. "I guess I was just worried about what people would think about me. I mean, it's different, having a donor. And Simon has this huge normal family."

"No family is 'normal,'" Samantha said.

"That's not what I meant," I said.

"Yeah, I know what you mean," Henry said. "Like when Andrew and I had to change schools because we moved to California, and people thought it was weird that we have two moms. But you know, that's just our life and we can't expect other people to accept it if we don't accept it ourselves."

"You sound like Mom," Andrew said as he rolled his eyes.

"No, really," Henry said. "We just had to accept it and not try to hide it. And pretty soon, everyone at school got used to it, so it's not a big deal anymore."

"Well, you guys are a big deal to me," I said. "But a big deal in a good way. I'm really glad you're here."

"Me too," Samantha said.

"Me too," Tate said. "It's cool here, and I have a new joke to tell you. Ready?"

"Ready," I said.

"Okay," he said. "How do porcupines play leapfrog?"

"I don't know. How?"

"Very carefully," Tate said. "Get it? Because they're so prickly, they have to be careful."

"I get it," I said. "That's a good one. I'll have to tell Charlie."

Grandma Diane came over to our table, and we all smiled so she could take a picture.

"You know that means you guys will be on next year's poster," I told them after Grandma Diane had walked away to take someone else's picture. "I hope you come to the Ross reunion every single year from now on. It's really cool to have my whole entire family all in one place."

We finished up our hot dogs. Simon came over and asked us if we wanted to play touch football with him and some of the cousins. Andrew, Henry, and Tate said they wanted to. Samantha and I picked up the paper plates to throw them away and walked around to the side of the field. I watched Simon divide everyone up into teams.

"Twenty-four, twenty-seven, hike one, hike two," Simon yelled out.

"You know what I've always wondered," Samantha said. "How do they know what numbers to say when they play football? They always say different numbers, and I can never figure it out."

"I have no idea," I told her. "But all the guys seem to know what to do." Andrew had the ball and was running across the grass. I thought how, if he was the kind of brother I lived with, I would've probably watched him in a hundred football games by now. I would probably know the names of all the kids on his team. Maybe I would even have made posters to hold up at the games. Or maybe I would just take him for granted, like lots of sisters did with their younger brothers.

Andrew made it to the end of the field and Henry high-fived him. "Go, Andrew!" Samantha shouted. "Woo hoo!"

He turned to Samantha and me and waved, and we waved back.

"That was a touchdown, right?" I asked.

"I think so," Samantha said. "I'm really not into football."

"Me either," I said.

"God, we're such girls," Samantha said.

"They have these paths through the woods over there," I told her, pointing across the field. "Do you want to take a walk or something?"

"Sure," she said. She linked her arm through mine and we walked around the picnic benches. Mom was sitting with Amy. She had baby Asher up on her shoulder, and she waved to me as we passed by.

"Hey, Leah. Leah!" Charlie called. "Where are you going?"

"Just for a little walk," I said.

"Can I come?" he asked. I hesitated for a second, since I kind of wanted it to just be Samantha and me. After all, we barely ever got to see each other. It was only the second time I'd ever seen her in person. "Please," Charlie said.

I turned to Samantha and shrugged. "Do you want a piggyback ride?" she asked him.

"Yes, please," he said.

Samantha bent down so Charlie could climb up on her back, and then she went racing ahead of me toward the trees. "Come on, Leah, come on!" Charlie cried.

We followed one of the paths in the woods. There are little signs along the path that label the trees—they're all named for people who have donated money to the park.

I'd been on the path about a hundred times, but Samantha never had, and she stopped in front of every little sign. Charlie asked Samantha to put him down, and he stepped up to one of the trees. "If I was Spider-Man, I could climb this," he said.

"That would be cool," I said.

He walked around to the other side of the tree, which was farther back from the path. "Come on back, Char," I said. "You know we're supposed to stay on the path."

He took one more step away. "Hey, Leah, do you think it's possible that no one ever stepped here before? Since it's not on the path? Do you think that maybe I'm the first person ever to step here?"

"I don't know," I said.

"I definitely think it's possible," Samantha said.

"Yeah, me too," Charlie said.

"All right," I said. "It's possible—now come back here!"

Charlie bounded back over to us. "Hey, Samantha, come on! I'll be Batman and you be Robin, and I'm saving you from the evil monster. Hurry up, it's chasing us!"

"Hurry up, Leah," Samantha said. "It's gaining on us!"

Charlie ran all the way to his favorite tree. It's his favorite because the little sign in the front says FOR CHARLES, and Charlie thinks that means it's his tree.

Charlie wrapped his arms around the trunk of the tree. "Leah, look, it's my tree. Just like in the poster you made. Now I have to interview Samantha," Charlie said.

"For what?" Samantha asked.

"My family tree," Charlie said, and then he turned to

me. "She's family, right? That's why she's at the family reunion."

"Right," I said. "But you know it's not Family Month anymore."

"No, it's State Month now," Charlie said. "But it's okay because we're in another state, so it can be like a combination."

"A combination?" I asked.

"Yeah, a combination Family and State Month," he said.

Charlie looked so cute right then. I loved the way he sounded when he used big words. I mean, what kind of five-year-old uses the word "combination"? "I love you, Charlie," I said.

"Love you too," Charlie said quickly, automatically. Then he turned to Samantha. "Leah helped me make my family tree so it's better than Aaron's, even though Leah said Aaron's the teacher's pet."

"Don't tell Mom that," I said.

"So now I have to interview you," Charlie said.

"What do you want to know?" Samantha asked.

"What's your favorite color?"

"Um, I think red."

"What's your favorite sport?"

"I don't really have a favorite, except maybe cheerleading. I'm trying out next year when I get to high school." I hadn't known that Samantha wanted to be a cheerleader. It sounded like something Avery would want to do. "What's your favorite sport?" she asked Charlie.

"I like bikes," he said. "Have you ever heard of Lance Armstrong?"

"He's a biker, right?"

"He's a cyclist," Charlie corrected. "But don't you think his name should be Lance *Leg*strong? I mean, he uses his legs mostly, not his arms, when he rides his bike."

"You're totally right about that," Samantha said.

"Hey, I felt a raindrop," Charlie said.

As soon as he said it, I felt a raindrop plop onto my arm, and then another on my head. And then they were falling all over us. "Come on, come on!" I said. The three of us raced back up the path to the rest of the family. We came out of the woods, and everything was all wet. Mom and Anna Holland were pulling the posters off the trees and rolling them up. Simon was still playing football in the rain with Andrew, Henry, and Tate, and a couple of the cousins were splashing in the puddles. Everyone else was huddled on the picnic benches with umbrellas over them. Grandma Diane was holding Asher tight to shield him from the rain.

"I don't think this will pass, Ma," Amy said. "Maybe we should move this to your house. Is that all right?"

"Of course. Rain is lucky anyhow," Grandma Diane said. "Didn't you know that? It's a very lucky thing if a bird poops in your hair or if it rains on your wedding day. So it must be lucky if it rains during a family reunion. As a matter of fact, I think that since it didn't rain until after we finished barbecuing, the rain is extra lucky."

"Mom's a real lemonade-out-of-lemons kind of woman," Amy said.

"I've just been lucky," she said.

I stood back and looked at my family, my whole family, all there together in the park. Simon threw the football to Tate. I heard him yell out, "Tate-man, what a catch!" Mom was bent in conversation with Anna Holland. Samantha was next to me, pulling her sweatshirt over her head to block out the rain. I felt lucky too. I decided I took after Simon's side of the family.

chaptereighteen

A few weeks later Mom's publisher called to say her book was ready to go and would be sent out to book-stores the next month. Mom says writing a book is kind of like having another kid—you worry about what it will look like and whether people will like it. You work as hard as you can to make it the best it can be, and then you send it off into the world and hope for the best. When it does well, you feel proud and happy. When it doesn't sell, you feel like it's all your fault and you're a complete and utter failure.

Mom's publisher always sends a few free copies of her books to our house before they're actually sent out to bookstores, and Mom told me I could invite Avery, Brenna, and Callie over for a little book party. She would read part of her book out loud to us, just like she does when she's on tour. Avery, Brenna, and Callie could even ask questions about it if they wanted. Then Mom would sign a copy of the book for each of them. She always writes little notes to people when she signs her books, like "Best Wishes" or "Good Luck on the SATs!" I wanted Samantha to come to the book party too, but she had a big history test the next week and Anna Holland said she absolutely had to stay in Haverford and study that weekend. But we made plans to get together the week that school let out for the summer, and Samantha was planning another donor sibling reunion for August. I really couldn't wait. I hadn't spent enough time with the boys at the reunion, and I wanted to get to know them better. We had started e-mailing one another every week. Tate e-mailed me jokes, just like Samantha said he would. Sometimes I told them to Charlie. And Andrew and Henry wrote me about the things they were up to. But still, e-mailing is not the same thing as getting to see your brothers in person. Mom said she would definitely let me visit everyone in August, and in the meantime she would sign a copy of the book for Samantha and send it to her in Haverford.

Anyway, I think the main reason Mom wanted me to invite people over is because she gets nervous whenever her books first come out, not just because it's like having another kid to worry about, but also because she has to go on tour and speak to strangers in bookstores. You'd think after being a writer for so many years, she'd be used to it and stop being so nervous, but she gets scared every time. She likes to practice reading passages before she actually has to be in front of a crowd of strangers, so reading in front of my friends would be a good warm-up before her tour.

Mom had arranged for Charlie to have a playdate with Aaron, so he wouldn't interrupt the reading or make us all watch *The Lion King* with him instead of listening to Mom. Avery, Brenna, and Callie came home with me after school.

We dropped our backpacks in the front hall. "Mom!" I yelled. "We're home!"

"I'll be there in a minute," Mom yelled back from the kitchen. "I'm just finishing up an e-mail."

We walked back toward the living room. I saw that Mom had put out chips and salsa on the coffee table. There was also a plate of carrots and celery because I'd told Mom that Brenna ate only healthy food. "I guess she's doing the reading in here," I said. "So, you know, make yourselves at home."

"Does it matter where we sit?" Brenna asked.

"I think my mom will sit in that chair," I said, pointing to a chair that was usually at the dining room table but was now set up facing the couch. "But we can sit anywhere else—on the couch, or the floor, or wherever."

Avery sat on the couch, but she was acting all fidgety. "This is awesome," she said. "I've never met a real author before."

"What are you talking about?" I said. "You've met my mom a bunch of times."

"I know," Avery said. "But she was just a mom then. Now she's a writer. I'm sort of nervous."

"You're crazy," I told her.

"Whatever," she said. "You love me anyway."

"So where's the book?" Callie asked.

"I don't know," I said. "I haven't even seen it yet. My mom's publisher was sending it overnight, and it was supposed to arrive this morning. I don't even know what the cover looks like. It's not going to be in stores until next month."

"I can't believe we get to see a book before it's even in

stores," Avery said. She bounced up and down a little, the way Charlie does when he's really excited about something on television. Brenna sank onto the couch next to Avery. "Aren't you excited?" Avery asked her.

"Yeah," Brenna said. "But I'm also so depressed!"

"What's the matter?"

"You know," Brenna said. "Chase."

"What about him?"

"That he's back with Lizzie," Brenna said, and she sighed loudly. "It's just so awful. I saw him walking down the hall with Lizzie. He had his arm around her shoulder. She was leaning up against him and you should have seen how he was looking at her. Like he was completely in love. His eyes were half-open, half-closed—you know, that dreamy look guys always get in the movies. Even though Lizzie's totally wrong for him!"

Avery had stopped bouncing and rolled her eyes. "What? And you're right for him?"

"I could be," Brenna said. "If he would just dump Lizzie for good, then maybe he would look at me like that." Brenna cocked her head and batted her eyelashes. "Don't you think he could love me?"

"That's how Ian looks at me sometimes," Callie said.

"You're so lucky," Brenna said. "Unrequited love is so tragic!"

"Oh, puh-lease," Avery said.

"Seriously," Brenna said. "It's really hard to love Chase so much and see him running after Lizzie instead of me. I just don't understand it. I mean, they're barely speaking half the time. I wouldn't fight with him like she does. He's so hot. What's there to fight about?"

"You are totally pathetic," Avery said.

"But it's true," Brenna insisted.

Avery looked at me and rolled her eyes again. I knew she thought it was really dumb that Brenna was always falling all over Chase. I guess it was kind of silly, but I sort of agreed with Brenna anyway, and I decided not to worry anymore if Avery thought I was being stupid too. After all, she was the one who told me you can't waste time worrying what other people think about you. "The thing is," I said, "Chase *is* really hot."

"Oh, no," Avery cried. "Not you, too!"

I shrugged my shoulders. "You see?" Brenna said. "He's irresistible!"

"Well, I have some news for you," Avery said. "Chase decided last night where he's going to college, and he's going to be geographically unavailable to you both."

"Where's he going?" I asked.

"Stanford."

"Is that in Connecticut?" Brenna asked.

"No, it's in California. It's practically the best school in the whole country too."

"Your dad must be happy," I said. "Even if it isn't Yale."

"Please," Avery said. "Now that Chase is planning to go to Stanford, Lizzie says she's going to go to college in California too. My dad's worried Chase is going to grow his hair really long and become a surfer. And then he and Lizzie will run off and get married, and have little surfer children." I pictured Chase in California, with his dark hair lightened from the sun and falling in front of his face the way it did when he was leaning over the stairwell.

"Well, *I* love California," Brenna said. "And my aunt Rose said I have a really strong love line." She waved her palm in front of Avery. "You see?" she said.

Avery squeezed her eyes shut and put her hands over her ears. "I can't take it anymore," she said. "When's your mom gonna come out here?"

I remembered something just then, and I held my palm out toward Brenna. "Hey, Brenna, can you check out my family line?"

"Huh?"

"My family line," I repeated. "Callie was telling us about you learning how to read palms when you were in New Mexico, but I can't remember which one was the family line."

"None of them," Brenna said. "There's no such thing as a family line."

Avery dropped her hands from her ears. "See, Callie, I told you so," she said.

Mom came out then, with a stack of books in her arms— one for each of us. "Hey, girls," she said. "Thanks so much for coming."

"Oh, thanks so much for having us," Avery said.

"My pleasure," Mom said. "I really need the practice." She handed us each a book. I ran my fingers across the cover. *How to Talk So Your Parents Will Listen* it said in bold blue letters. Above the title, in a different shade of blue, it said "Meredith Hoffman-Ross." The letters in Mom's name were raised up slightly.

"This is so unbelievably cool," Avery said.

"The cover looks really good," I told Mom.

"Open it up," Mom said. "There's a surprise for you."

"What do you mean?"

"Just open it," Mom said. "You'll see."

I opened it carefully so I wouldn't break the binding. It had that brand-new-book smell, and the pages were crisp and white. I wasn't sure what I was supposed to be looking for, but I turned the pages slowly—past the title page and the copyright page. And then I saw it: "*Dedicated to my wonderful daughter, Leah Isabel Hoffman-Ross, who taught me how to listen.*" "You dedicated it to me?" I asked. "Really?"

Mom nodded.

"But I thought you didn't believe in dedicating books to your kids," I said.

"I've been rethinking a lot of things lately," Mom said.

"Oh, Leah," Avery said. "I can't believe your name is in an actual book—like, anyone can just go to a bookstore and buy this book, and there's your name right there. It's just so awesome. Your mom is so awesome."

I was looking across the room at Mom as I answered Avery. There was no other mother I could ever want more. There was no other family that I wanted to be part of. "I know," I said.

Here's a sneak peek at *Positively*, the new novel
by Courtney Sheinmel.

All Emerson Price wants is to be normal. But ever
since the day she and her mother were diagnosed as
HIV-positive, nothing has felt very normal at all. Now
Emmy's mom is dead, and Emmy can't imagine living without her. No one else, not even her best friend,
understands what it's like to have to take medicine
every single day, and to be so afraid of getting sick.
Emmy has never felt so alone.

When Emmy's dad and his new wife send her to
Camp Positive, a camp for HIV-positive girls, Emmy
is sure that she is going to hate it. But soon Emmy
begins to realize that she's not alone after all—and that
sometimes, letting other people in can make all the
difference in the world.

Chapter 1

When my mother died I imagined God was thinking, "One down, and one to go."

We were an ordinary family up until Mom got sick. I don't really remember what it was like to be ordinary, since I was only four years old when it all changed. Most of my life I've been different from everybody else.

But sometimes I look at the pictures of us from before. A regular family. A mom, a dad, a little girl. I can tell when Mom was getting sick by how old I look in the pictures, and whether or not I have bangs. The first time Mom got really sick was right around the time I started to grow out my bangs, so my favorite pictures are the ones where I still have bangs and I know for sure that she was healthy. When my bangs are too long and clipped back from my forehead, I know that means Mom is closer to dying.

I don't remember the first time Mom told me she was sick, and that I could get sick too. It seems like something I've always known. At first, Mom just had a cold. It wasn't a big deal, because people get colds all the time, even though Mom was the kind of person who never got sick. But I was in preschool, so she thought maybe I'd brought home germs from the other kids and given them to her. She figured it was just a normal cold like regular people get. Except Mom's cold just wouldn't go away. She went to the doctor and he put her on antibiotics and said it should clear up in a few days, but Mom got worse. One night she couldn't breathe at all, and Dad rushed her to the hospital. It turned out she had pneumonia, but it was more than that. The doctors at the hospital said the reason Mom had pneumonia was because she also had a disease called AIDS. They said Dad and I also had to be tested to see if we were infected with it too. Dad wasn't, but I was. They figured out that Mom had gotten infected before I was born, and I got it when she was pregnant with me.

Mom went on special medication for people with AIDS, and she got better for a while. Even though I wasn't sick, the doctors said I could get sick at any time because I was HIV-positive, which means the virus that causes AIDS is in my blood. From then on, Mom and I had to go to the doctor every couple of months. They tested our blood for things called viral loads and T-cells. If our viral loads were high and our T-cell levels were low, it meant we could be really sick. My blood was drawn so many times I wondered if I would eventually run out. Every time Mom or I got a cold or a stomachache, we had to go to the doctor to make sure it wasn't something worse. After a while, I started having to take the medication too. Sometimes Mom would look at me and start to cry, but usually she pretended she wasn't crying. She would say something dumb, like there was something in her eye or she was remembering a sad movie.

The last thing Mom said to me was "I love you to the sky." It was this game we used to play from when I was little. "Do you love me to the top of my head?" I'd ask. "Higher," Mom would say. "Do you love me to the top of that tree?" "Even higher." "Do you love me to the roof?" "Higher than that." "How high do you love me?" I'd finally ask, and Mom would say, "I love you to the sky."

She died on a Tuesday morning. Afterward the men from the funeral home came to take her body away, and Mom's friend Lisa took me outside. It was too hard to breathe in the house, but the air outside was cool and crisp. It was April, and we sat on the lawn in front of the house. I bent my legs and rested my chin on top of my knees. It had happened way too fast. She was coughing and coughing for months, but she didn't seem that sick. And then all of a sudden she was really sick. My parents had divorced when I was eight years old, so my dad didn't live with us anymore. When Mom got too sick for us to live on our own, different people came to stay. Mom's father came up to Connecticut from Florida; then her sister, my aunt Laura, came in from Colorado. The last two weeks Lisa had come. And we had nurses in and out of the house. But I still didn't really believe that Mom would actually ever die. Even after it happened, I wasn't sure I believed it. I always thought that we would be all right, just because I couldn't imagine it any other way.

Lisa put her hand on my head. I had known her my whole life. She and my mother were best friends from college. I pretended it was Mom's fingers running though my hair. Lisa was pulling at a knot in my hair and my mother was dead. I could hear the ordinary, everyday sounds—wheels against pavement, wind rustling the leaves in the trees. A car drove by, like it was any other day. Why was everything still moving? I felt like everything should have stopped. How was I still breathing? I sucked in my breath and held it to see if it was possible to make time stop, but I could still feel my heart beating in my chest and I let my breath out slowly.

"What can I do, Emmy?" Lisa asked.

I didn't answer. *Mommy*, I said to myself silently, matching up the word to the beats in my chest. *Mom-my, Mom-my, Mom-my*. I said it over and over again in my head, like I was calling out to her. *Mommy*. It was a weird word. It was two words put together, like a compound word: "Mom" and "me." As if we were connected, even though there wouldn't ever be a mom and me again.

I thought about who I was right then, on the last day I had a mother. I had just turned thirteen. I was finishing up seventh grade. I was on the short side; my hair was just past my shoulders. That was how she knew me. The problem is, when someone dies, you keep growing. Things about me would change and she wouldn't be there to see them.

And what if I forgot things about her? My grandmother had died when I was nine, and there were things about her I couldn't remember. Like her voice. I couldn't remember anything about it, not even how she sounded when she said my name.

Sitting on the grass with Lisa, I could still hear Mom's voice in my head. I closed my eyes and could hear her saying my name. I decided to practice remembering it every day so I wouldn't ever forget it.

"Emmy," Lisa said, and I opened my eyes. "I spoke to your father. He said he wants to come over, but I told him I needed to ask you."

I thought of my father driving up our block in his white sedan and pulling into the driveway behind Mom's red car. "No," I said. "I don't want him to come here."

It didn't seem right for Dad to be at Mom's house. After all, he had divorced Mom. He had a new wife, and they were even having a baby. Mom had wanted to have another baby after me. I had heard her once talking about it with Lisa. She wanted me to be a big sister, but then she was diagnosed with AIDS. Now Dad was having a baby without her. "I wonder if he even cares that she's dead," I said.

"Oh, Emmy," Lisa said. "Of course he does."

I knew Lisa was probably right, but I didn't want to think about Dad anymore. There would be plenty of time for him. I used to see him only every other weekend and for dinner on Tuesday nights. The last couple of months I hadn't seen him as much because Mom didn't feel well and I was spending time with her. Anyway it didn't matter because now I'd be living with him . . . and with Meg, my stepmother, his new wife. I hated thinking about her as my father's wife, since that's what Mom used to be.

I wanted to concentrate on Mom and no one else. I tried to hold a picture of her up in my mind. I was full of Mom, but Mom was gone, so I was full of emptiness. It felt like something sharp was pressing behind my eyes. I squeezed them shut but they still felt raw and open. What happens when you die? Did Mom get to see her mother? I didn't want Mom to be alone, but I didn't want anyone else to get to be with her. I still needed Mom with me. I hooked my arms around my legs like I was hugging them. Lisa moved closer to me so there was hardly any space between us. "It's all right to cry," she said.

I pressed my face hard into my knees. The top of my jeans felt sticky. The inside of my chest hurt like it was bleeding. Was that what it meant to be bleeding internally? I hated blood. I always tried to stay away from sharp things so I wouldn't get cut and start bleeding. Seeing blood always reminded me that I was infected, and most of all I hated this stupid disease. I was curled into a ball and Lisa rocked and rocked me. It was getting cooler. During the day the sun beats down on our front lawn, but the sun had already moved, so it was behind the house and we were sitting in the shade. Soon it would be dark. I didn't want the day to end. At least today I had seen my mother. But tomorrow I wouldn't see her at all, or the day after that, or the day after that, or ever again. I made myself say it in my head: *You will never see Mom again.* I kept my face pressed against my knees for as long as I could, until all the snot and tears made it hard to breathe, and on top of that, I had to pee. I hadn't been to the bathroom since Mom had died. It seemed ridiculous to have to sit up and blow my nose and go to the bathroom. How could I still have to do things like that? I knew later on Lisa would try and make me eat dinner so I could take my pills without getting nauseous, and then I would brush my teeth and change my clothes and get into my bed.

There were so many things to do. I had to keep breathing, and I would have to put things into my mouth and chew and swallow. And I would have to go to the bathroom and go to school. None of it made any sense, since Mom was gone.

And then there were the other things we would have to do because we were still living and Mom was not, like pack everything up and give things away. Right now all of Mom's clothes were still in the big closet in her bedroom. But it would all get packed up. My stuff would be packed up too. The pictures would be taken off the walls. Lisa would go back to New York City, where she lived, and I would go to Dad and Meg's house.

Technically Dad and Meg's house would be my house now too. But *home* was where all Mom's stuff was—the furniture, the pictures. I wasn't sure where I would put all the pictures of Mom. I knew Meg wouldn't want me putting them up on the walls around Dad's house. And what about the rest of Mom's stuff? I wondered how I would squeeze everything important from Mom's house into my one little room at Dad's. We wouldn't have crunchy peanut butter in the fridge anymore. That was something only Mom liked.

From now on, everything I did would be things I did without a mother. No matter how much I wanted her. No matter how much I needed her. Mom was the only one who knew what it was like to have to take pills every day, and to be scared of getting sick, and to feel different. Now I would have to miss Mom too, and I wouldn't even have her to help me. It wasn't fair.

I didn't want to go back in the house without Mom. But I really had to pee. I lifted up my head and wiped my nose with my sleeve, just like a little kid. My mother was the kind of person who always had tissues in her purse. I turned back to Lisa. "I wish you could live here forever," I told her. If Lisa stayed, I could still live in my house. We wouldn't have to clean out Mom's closet or take all of the pictures off the walls. I thought maybe if I said it out loud, it would come true, even though I knew really it was impossible. Lisa lived so far away. She had a husband and a baby. Her husband called every day to check in. I knew he wanted her to go back home.

"Oh, Em, I know," Lisa said. "I'm so sorry."

"How long are you staying?"

"I'll be here until the end of the week," she said.

Did the end of the week mean Friday or Sunday? Friday was only three days away. I really hoped she meant Sunday. Then I thought it was awful of me to be worrying about the difference between Friday and Sunday. My mother had just died, after all.

"Can I stay here with you until you have to leave?" I asked.

"Absolutely," Lisa said.

"I have to go to the bathroom," I told her. I stood up and watched Lisa push herself up from the ground. She wiped her palms on her jeans and put her arm back around my shoulder. We walked up the steps and into the house together. *This is the first time I'm walking into my house without having a mother*, I thought, and then I stepped inside.

Read more about girls like you!

The Mother-Daughter Book Club
by Heather Vogel Frederick

I Wanna Be Your Shoebox
by Cristina García

The Truth About My Bat Mitzvah
by Nora Raleigh Baskin

The Teashop Girls
by Laura Schaefer

My So-Called Family
by Courtney Sheinmel

Published by Simon & Schuster Books for Young Readers
KIDS.SimonandSchuster.com

For fun. For inspiration. For you.
Atheneum.

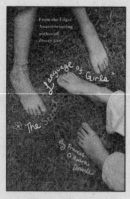

The Secret Language of Girls
by Frances O'Roark Dowell

Kira-Kira
by Cynthia Kadohata

The Higher Power of Lucky
by Susan Patron

Beneath My Mother's Feet
by Amjed Qamar

Standing for Socks
by Elissa Brent Weissman

Here's How I See It—
Here's How It Is
by Heather Henson

Atheneum Books for Young Readers * Published by Simon & Schuster